ing

e Changeling Three Changeling

Stillness of the Sea

by Nicol Ljubić

translated by Anna Paterson

Vagabond Voices
Glasgow

This translation was supported by
a grant from the Goethe-Institut
that is funded by the Ministry of
Foreign Affairs.

Printed and bound by Thomson Litho, East Kilbride

Cover design by Freight Design, Glasgow

For further information on Vagabond Voices, see the website,
www.vagabondvoices.co.uk

Stillness of the Sea

Prologue

The Hague, December

"Your Honours, before I address you on the subject of the crime, I would like to give you a brief account of the historical context within which it was committed. Until 1991, the former Yugoslavia was a federal republic made up of six constituent republican states. The death of Marshal Tito, head of state, led to the threat of complete breakdown in the country. The Yugoslav People's Army intervened, at first in Slovenia, then in Croatia and finally in Bosnia, with the intention of creating a new state from these bloody conflicts. In the midst of the seceding nations, a new Yugoslavia was to be forged around two of the republics, inhabited by Serbs and Montenegrins – Montenegro being Serbia's closest ally. Senior politicians in Serbia and Bosnia hatched this plan, which the Yugoslav People's Army carried out with a complete lack of moral restraint, while also relying on special units under the control of the Serbian Ministry for Internal Affairs and paramilitary groups financed by the nationalist parties, acting as go-betweens for local politicians and police headquarters. The Serb forces carried out their military operations in a coordinated and systematic manner until, by the end of 1992, the campaign had resulted in the murder or forced resettlement of some two million non-Serbian citizens.

One particular case brought the town of Višegrad grim notoriety.

Before the war reached Bosnia, Višegrad was a small town in eastern Bosnia and Herzegovina. One of several communities on the shore of the River Drina, it now belongs to Republika Srpska.

During the war, numerous factors conferred strategic importance upon the town. One of these was the large hydroelectric station at a dam located in the municipality. The dam served not only to generate energy, but also to control the water level in the river and thus prevent flooding. A second factor was Višegrad's position on a major traffic route, which is the crucial road link between Belgrade and Sarajevo.

On 6th April 1992, locally recruited Serb units began shelling the town and the surrounding villages, principally targeting the Muslim villages and residential areas. A small group of vengeful Muslims occupied the dam and threatened to blow it up. One of them succeeded in opening the gates sufficiently to cause flooding of some houses and streets, with the result that many civilians, Muslims and Serbs, fled from the town. Units of the Yugoslav People's Army moved in and established control of the dam and, soon afterwards, the town as well.

Army representatives told the Muslim spokesmen that no one had anything to fear from the soldiers and, reassured, they called their fellow citizens back from their hiding places and advised them to return to their homes. Many trusted these assurances and followed the advice. This was to have appalling consequences. Policemen and paramilitary militiamen robbed them and threatened to kill them. Muslims holding important posts in the town were allowed to go, though some of them disappeared. Paramilitary units drove through the streets with loudspeakers mounted on their cars, broadcasting recorded torture sessions.

The situation deteriorated further when the Yugoslav army withdrew from the town. Once the soldiers had left, the leaders of the local Serbs designated Višegrad a Serbian town and took over the running of the local authority. They organised training camps where the men were taught how to use guns. Before long, the Serb citizenry were ready to join the police and the paramilitaries in the execution of one of the most brutal ethnic cleansing actions of the Bosnian war. Muslims were to be cleared out of the town forever.

Hundreds of unarmed Muslim civilians were killed in Višegrad. The dead bodies of men, women and children were thrown into the Drina after being murdered on the riverbank or the ancient Turkish bridge – a historic symbol of the smouldering hostility between Serbs and Muslims. The current carried the savagely mutilated corpses down the river and deposited them on the bank near the village of Slap, where the Drina forms a great loop. Muslims who did not fall victim to murder were imprisoned. They were beaten, tortured and sexually abused. Many of them died. The town had two mosques and both were completely destroyed.

In the Balkan war, Višegrad is one of the most striking examples of successful ethnic cleansing.

Muslims made up over 61 per cent of the town's population of twenty-one thousand. According to records compiled by the Red Cross, twelve thousand inhabitants were either forced to leave or murdered. It is Višegrad's heartbreaking claim to fame that in no other community – except Srebrenica – have so many human beings disappeared, principally young adult males. These are facts that you should keep in mind during the days, weeks or months that might pass before a verdict is reached in this trial.

It is my belief that this short introduction was necessary to provide you with some understanding of the circumstances which pertained at the time when the man who now appears before you took part in a vicious crime."

A slight breeze rippled the sea, which recovered its smoothness close to the beach. The flow of air came off the water, passing over the wide Baltic beach and the two of them, and then on through the dune grasses. They lay still, with closed eyes. "How do you say that the sea is calm?" she asked. He didn't understand what she meant. When the sea is calm, it's calm. Or still, perhaps. "So, you have no word for it?" she queried. "In my language there is a word."

He can hear her voice. Very clear, a little too deep. He recalls the face that goes with the timbre of her voice. Serious eyes, high cheekbones, a narrow nose, a forehead with a few wrinkles and pale, almost anaemic-looking skin, framed by dark hair. From above, he observes the imprint of his body in the sand, but she has left no mark next to his. He can't explain it. Perhaps the sand was too firm and she too light. How can that be? Was it reasonable that some people should leave no trace in the sand? Not even in one's imagination? She was lying next to him, he is certain of that. But he doesn't know for how long. He could sense the tips of her hair, her long, dark hair, touching his face and tickling it.

He opened his eyes. She had been bending over him. Seen from above, it must have looked as if she were kissing him. She placed her hands on his face, hands that were always so cold. *"Bonaca."* The word locked into his mind. Seastillness.

He is one of the last to enter the public gallery. A guard hands him a set of headphones and points to one of the few free seats. He goes to sit in the third row, next to a group of young people who, he guesses, must be students because all of them have a notepad open.

A low murmur coming from the headphones fills the air. He examines the courtroom through the pane of bullet-proof glass. Three black-robed judges, then a row of clerks of the court, the prosecutor on the right and, on the left, a phalanx of defence lawyers seated in front of the defendant, who wears a dark suit, a white shirt and a tie. His thick, black hair is unusual for a man of his age; he is sixty years old. His forehead is high and his shapely, slender nose makes his face look almost gentle. Two blue-uniformed guards, who are relieved at regular intervals, stand close by, keeping a watchful eye on him.

The presiding judge, a thin, elderly man with white hair, turns to the prosecutor, a Mr Bloom, and asks him to complete the plea for the prosecution in the three hours that remain before the court will withdraw for lunch. The prosecutor – a tall, handsome man, whose robe sits tightly across his broad shoulders – rises, glances at the defendant, and begins to speak. At first, the interpreter interrupts a few times to tell him to stand closer to the microphone.

From where he is sitting in the public gallery, Mr Bloom's back is turned to him most of the time.

"You will grasp the extent of her suffering when you see the pain in her eyes and the scars left on her face by that night of fire. You may find her voice too faint and fail to understand everything she says. You will doubt if this woman can be telling the truth, because her truthfulness will make you question your ideas about humanity. She will try to give an account of that night and the unspeakable crime of which she is the sole survivor. I assume that you all understand the courage that this woman has had to summon up and the agony she has endured at the prospect of coming here to speak out in front of you all, and in the presence of this man, whom she has met only once before: on the night when her family, the Hasanovićs, were burnt to death."

The defendant slips his headphones off for a few minutes and inspects the nails on his left hand, starting with the little finger. Then he rubs his hands together, only to stop suddenly, as if it took him just that brief moment to realise how cynical it made him look, in this setting.

He watches the defendant from behind the glass screen, and is unable to take his eyes off him. At the same time, he wishes he could hate this man just as much as the others in the public gallery do – people who are less familiar with his name. Sensing his breath flow between his lips and the tip of his tongue, he realises that he is soundlessly forming the letters of that name: Zlatko Šimić. He looks around anxiously, but the young woman next to him has put on her headphones and isn't looking his way.

"This man claimed that he was a Red Cross worker, showed the family documentation and then ushered them into the house in which they were later to be burnt alive. All forty-two relatives of the woman who stands before you died in that fire – her parents, grandparents, aunts, uncles and cousins, her three sisters and her baby brother, just two days old. The man had told them that they would be safe in the house and that buses would arrive in the morning to take them out of town. By then, there was nothing the Hasanovićs wanted more than to escape from the place that had for so long been their home – until their own neighbours drove them out. They were the last Muslims in the entire village to abandon their houses. On 14th June 1992, they crossed the old Višegrad bridge in search of the Red Cross station. The family's great tragedy began when, as a result of this expedition, they crossed the path of this man, who has told this court that his name is Zlatko Šimić. He has declared himself innocent of the charges brought against him. He will assert that he had been admitted to the Višegrad hospital for treatment at the time the crime was committed. In evidence, the defence will produce a copy of the admission record. This forces us to draw the conclusion that either he or she is telling the truth, that either the defendant or this witness is lying to this court. It is your task to decide which you believe, him or her. In doing this, you must be aware of what it has meant for this woman to appear before the court today and speak of the night when her relatives died in the fire. She will have to live through those events one more time. You should also keep in mind the risks she has taken in coming to the court and you must look into her eyes. Then you will realise that this woman cannot be lying."

Eyes are the window to the soul, or so it is said. He asks himself if he ever truly looked into her eyes. He loved her eyes so much, but if he had looked closely, might they not have revealed something else – a lie, perhaps, or shadows cast by a life routinely hidden from him? He could not see the defendant's eyes; he was too far away. But would he trust himself to meet them, if they ever came face to face?

"True enough, this man is not the vilest of all defendants who have ever appeared before this court, in that he is not someone who murdered with his own hands, nor was he the one who struck the match and let it drop. His crime began when he offered to help these desperate people, led them to the house already soaked in an inflammable liquid and assured them that buses would be ready for them in the morning. This is the man who locked them into the house and stayed on the spot until two men arrived – two men he knew well. These men robbed the Hasanovićs of their money, watches and jewellery and forced every one of them to undress. Next, one of the men struck a match and let it drop. The house instantly went up in flames. They locked the door and, for about two hours, waited in front of the building until the screaming had finished. You look at him now, this man, who with aforethought led forty-two human beings, most of them women and children, to their death; this man, for whom the fire clearly was not enough. The following morning, he had pigs brought to the site and made sties for them out of the remains of the house. Such a calculated gesture: pigs!"

He stands very still, his gaze fixed on his notes. His accusations are stated in a surprisingly calm tone of voice and without urgency, even when the passages might have caused him to display some emotion.

"Perhaps you cannot imagine quite how hard it will be for the young woman to appear here as a witness and testify. Memories from that night will forever torment her, but even so, running through such images in one's mind is not the same thing as having to find words to describe them. You should consider this when she is called to the witness box to stand before you. And remember this too: she was fourteen years old on the night she was robbed of everyone she loved."

Now and then, Zlatko Šimić tilts his chair back so that it leans against the wall. At one point, he takes a comb from his jacket pocket to tidy his parting; from time to time he plays with the end of his tie, winding it around his finger and then smoothing the material out again. When he lets his eyes scan the hall, they never stay on anyone in particular, as if he refuses to accept that these are the people sitting in judgement over him or watching him being judged from behind the glass screen.

Šimić's lawyers keep taking notes and passing pieces of paper to each other. The judges sit still. One of them puts his elbow on the armrest and leans his head on his hand.

He takes the headphones off and hears once more the subdued murmur from all the other ones. He looks around. Practically everyone is following the trial, intent, fascinated. An elderly lady begins to cry. She wipes her eyes with a hanky.

He thinks of how much easier it would have been for him if she too had wept just once – if he had seen her tears and comforted her. He would have hugged her, or maybe stemmed her tears with his finger, wiping them away. Now, he wishes it intensely. Why isn't she here at least, sitting next to him? Why not be here together?

The young woman next to him has already filled several pages of her notebook. He studies her slender wrist as it rests on the small desktop and watches the play of fragile bones beneath the pale skin on the back of her hand.

Then, through the glass, he notes Mr Bloom making a gesture in the direction of the defendant, like a silent invitation.

How could Šimić just sit there so impassively?

A woman starts to curse. So far, he has taken no notice of her. The guard, who all this time has been standing behind the rows of seats, comes along and tells her to be quiet. The woman removes her headphones and speaks in English. "He's such an animal. Do you understand what I'm saying?" The guard replies: "Please, you must leave the room." He waves towards the door. A few people turn to watch, some of them scornfully, others sympathetically. The woman breathes in – it sounds like a sigh – then puts her headphones back on.

He resumes his observation of his neighbour's hand and the mechanical shifting of bones. The sight calms him. He has a vision of tiny piano hammers soundlessly hitting the strings. Then he too pulls his headphones on.

The judge asks the prosecutor for the name of the house where the crime took place, because it has become confused with another. There was a second house, also in Pionirska Street, in which other people had been burnt alive. The question of the number of the house is raised. But in this instance, the house had no number as, he points out, is unfortunately quite common in those parts. Mr Bloom suggests that, because the house belonged to the Memićs, it should be referred to as the Memić house, but the judges disapprove, arguing that it is too difficult to keep track of names. Instead, they agree to call it the House by the Stream. At this point, the presiding judge announces the midday break.

The public must clear the courtroom and go downstairs to the lobby. The guard addresses him as he is about to leave the public gallery. He should stand when the judges rise. Everyone in the courtroom has to and that means members of the public too, the guard points out adding, "It's to show respect." He doesn't know what to say. He nods and goes out without looking back.

The lobby is two floors down. The few armchairs are already occupied. He crosses over to the water dispenser, fills a beaker and takes it outside. It is snowing now. Above the roofs, the sky is a wintry grey. He is the only one to go out.

He stayed in his seat to see Šimić being escorted out and, as the last one to leave the courtroom, watched the defence lawyers pull off their black robes. One of them wiped his brow with a handkerchief, and another got a salami roll out of his briefcase. Behind their backs, Šimić was led away by the two guards. Their route took them in the direction of the public gallery and when for a brief moment he had the impression that Šimić was coming towards him, he felt like ducking to hide behind the seats in the row in front.

He arrived in The Hague on the evening of the previous day, after nearly eight hours on the train. At first, he sat by a window, absent-mindedly leafing through the magazines and the book he had bought for the journey, until just after Hanover, when he put them down on the seat next to his. From then on, he stared out at the flat landscape, the bare trees and brown fields, their furrows outlined by a crust of snow. For long stretches, there were hardly any houses, not even a farmstead. A road, field tracks and grey clouds gathering in the sky. It rained intermittently.

He sought out a hotel on the shore. He wanted a room with a view of the sea. The receptionist asked him how long he would be staying, but he had no idea what to tell her. "I don't know," he said, "four nights, perhaps five. Perhaps more."

The train stopped once, owing to "an accident involving a man on the line", as the announcement put it. A man behind him had been outraged. People should top themselves at home, if that's what they want, he said. There are plenty of ways to go about it. No one contradicted him.

They were kept waiting for an hour, stuck in the empty landscape. By the time the train finally started moving, the person who had killed himself had vanished from his thoughts. Everyone left thoughts of the dead man behind. Ana couldn't do that, he suddenly realised. Forty-two dead bodies, forty-two anguished deaths. And now here is the accused, who keeps smoothing his tie. He was expecting another kind of man – someone broken, with grief-stricken eyes, pale skin and hollow cheeks.

He would like to know whether Ana would consider this an appropriate image. But they didn't talk, and haven't seen each other since. He doesn't know if that was the end or not. He doesn't know what had held her back, why she hadn't told him earlier. Why couldn't she confide in him? He often fails to understand why she decided to tell him anything at all.

Afterwards, during all of the last three weeks, he has tried to distance himself from her. And he tried to distance himself from her life story too, but soon found this impossible.

She didn't know of his journey to The Hague. For a long time, he thought a great deal about whether or not he should go, but was persuaded in the end that it might be of use to him, to them both perhaps. It might at least help him to understand a little better. Now, after the first hour in court, he is doubtful. Instead, he is anguished by the thought that Ana might come to seem alien to him, and so too his love for her. For the first time, he is also fearful that he might find something appealing about that man, so obviously unmoved by his surroundings. Even if it were only some small thing, like an old man's freckle on his forehead, a timid gesture, a brief attack of weakness, or perhaps simply something like the way he folded his handkerchief after blowing his nose.

The young witness has taken her seat in the courtroom, and her back in a mint-green cardigan is turned to the public gallery. Her black hair touches her shoulders. On the screen mounted above the protective glass, he can see her face with its scarred right side. She sits there, calm and collected, at least that is how she seems to the onlooker and he asks himself how this can be possible – how does she manage? She has kept her eyes averted from Šimić, and even when she entered the room, her gaze shifted immediately to find the chair where she was to sit.

The presiding judge asks her to stand to take the oath. She swears in the name of God to speak the truth and nothing but the truth. The judge tells her to sit down and hands the proceedings over to Mr Bloom, who rises and turns to his witness.

"I would like you to begin by stating the name of the community where you once lived."

"I lived in Koritnik, six kilometres outside Višegrad."

Her steady voice and brisk, firm delivery surprise him.

"How do you earn your livelihood?"

"I'm a nurse."

"To what ethnic group do you belong?"

"I am a Muslim."

"Please tell the court what happened on the morning of the 14th of June 1992."

"One of our Serb neighbours had threatened us. We were all to be killed. That was why my parents decided to leave Koritnik"

"How many people were involved?"

"Altogether, almost fifty. I don't know the exact number."

"Was everyone in the group civilian?"

"Yes, everyone."

The defence lawyers are back to shuffling notes, the judges slump in their seats. Šimić stares at the table in front of him. Mr Bloom glances at his documents.

"Did the group include a newborn infant?"

"Yes, it did. He had been born forty-eight hours earlier. My little brother."

"Once you had arrived in Višegrad, where did you go?"

"We went to the police station. One of my uncles spoke to a policeman and told him that we wanted to find the Red Cross. The policeman informed him that the Red Cross was based in the hotel on the Drina, that we were to avoid the main street and stay together, all of us, but in twos."

"What happened next?"

"When we reached the bridge, we met a man who told us that the buses had already left. He worked for the Red Cross, he said, and was dealing with the refugees. He added that he could take us to a place where we could stay the night. The buses would be back the following day."

Mr Bloom pauses and looks at her fixedly.

"Do you think you would recognise the man if you were to see him again?"

"Yes, I'd recognise him. Only death could prevent me from doing that. The man is over there, that's him."

She gestures towards Šimić.

"Can you describe where in this room you see him?"

"Yes, I can. He is sitting on my left. I have not looked at him properly, so I cannot tell you what he is wearing. I would rather not see him at all."

"I would like you to look at him now, please, and assure the court that this man you are referring to is indeed the same man whom you met on the 14th of June 1992."

"He is seated behind that man there."

"Can you describe his clothes?"

"Something brown, I think. It's hard to be precise at this distance. Yes, it's brown. By now, he is sixteen years older than he was. He was better-looking, then."

She only casts a quick look at Šimić, hardly moves her head and avoids meeting his eyes.

What might have gone through her mind just then? He would have liked to know and so much wanted to ask her: what do you feel in the presence of this man?

Do you hate him?

But it's not that simple, hate is a word, a powerless word if used by people who have not yet experienced what it's like to hate. Hatred is different from love. One way or another, everyone has loved, but who would demand the right to judge the intensity of another love? I hate him because he has run off with my wife – yes, perhaps that's a kind of hatred, but what word am I to use? I watched as my entire family was burnt to death. I heard their screams. To this day, I still hear them.

Tell me, what do you feel?

Everyone who asks about this wants to know what I feel. Do I feel anything but hatred?

And?

Listen, he didn't keep his word. Maybe this is hard to understand, but that's what I can't help thinking about, all the time. Whenever I think of him at all.

Mr Bloom: "Your Honours, please note the witness's identification of the defendant."

Throughout, he has been listening to the voice of the English interpreter, a woman of indeterminate age, or so it seems to him. He imagines the interpreter following the trial in her sound-insulated booth. He tries to discern emotion in her voice – rage or grief – asking himself how she manages to translate all this without taking sides. He changes channel and listens to the witness. He can't understand what she is saying, and yet it seems so familiar he believes he can recognise certain words. But she is speaking too quickly for him to make sense of what she says, and he changes back to the earlier channel. He needs the translation in order to understand her.

"Can you recall what the defendant told you all next?"

"Yes. He said that he was a Red Cross official and responsible for explaining to refugees that they were safe and should feel at ease. No one would be allowed to harm us and no one would try either. But he advised us to stay together as a group."

"Did you observe him writing anything down?"

"He tore a sheet off a writing pad and wrote something down. I don't know what it was. He handed the note to my uncle, who showed it around. It apparently said that we were to be left alone and that no one should attack us. If anyone turned up, we were supposed to hand over the note."

"After your arrival at the House by the Stream, did some men turn up?"

"Yes, about an hour later. We had prayed to God and cooked a meal, so it must have been an hour or so afterwards, but I couldn't say exactly."

"Did you recognise these men?"

"I didn't dare to look at them. I heard their voices in front of the house, but only three of them came inside.

"I need to step away for a moment. Please excuse me."

Mr Bloom turns to the judges, exchanges a few words and then the older, white-haired judge nods.

The witness straightens up, as if she has only just realised how much her body has sunk into itself while she was being questioned. Her shoulders were sagging and bending her forward; her head was sinking slightly. Absorbed by her voice and the determined look on her face, he failed to notice when her body began to contradict her expression. Now, she seems desperate for a short break to recover.

She takes the headphones off, closes her eyes for a moment and presses her fingertips against her temples. Twice, her shoulders heave visibly as she takes deep breaths. Then she puts the headphones back on and speaks again.

"When they came inside the house, one of them ordered us to go into the next room. He wanted cash. Money and gold. He pulled a knife from his boot and said: 'I'll use it if I find someone has kept back a single dinar. Get on with it.'"

"What happened next?"

"We went into another room and the adults put all their money and jewellery on a table. One of the men was sitting on an armchair with a shotgun in his lap. He called to three of us and said: 'Get undressed.'"

"Were you one of the three?"

"Yes, I was."

"Then, what?"

"He said: 'Take your clothes off.' I began to unbutton my blouse. Then I said: 'I can't carry on.' He repeated: 'Undress. Like that.'"

"You held up your index finger just now. Was that how the man gestured to you?"

She breathes in. He knows this from the way her shoulders move.

"Yes. He showed me his index finger and said: 'You should be as naked as this finger.'"

Mr Bloom: "Please, continue."

"I began to take off my underwear. I had to come over to stand in front of him, then turn around. He looked at me. After a while, he said: 'Get dressed again!'"

"Where was the defendant at this time?"

"I don't know. Maybe he was waiting outside."

"Did one of the women refuse to take her clothes off?"

"Yes."

"Who was that?"

"My mother."

"What was done to her?"

"She had told the man that she didn't intend to undress. But my aunt caught hold of her and I started unbuttoning her blouse. Together, we undressed her."

The elderly lady who had been tearful earlier crosses herself.

"Were you all searched?"

"Yes. They searched everyone, even felt the children's pockets. One mother had put some things made of gold in her little son's pockets, I don't know exactly, but anyway they found out and beat him."

She makes as if hitting out with her fist.

Mr Bloom: "You show us a blow with your fist. Is that what the man did to the child?"

The witness: "Yes, it is. He hit the child in the face."

Some of the public shake their heads. The woman next to him has stopped taking notes, her fingers rest on the pad, closed round the pen. For a moment, everyone seems still, quiet. Even the interpreter.

Šimić fiddles with his suit buttons, twisting them.

The prosecutor looks down, puts one sheet of paper on top of another, then turns back to his witness.

"Did the men return later?"

"Yes. Yes, of course they did. Had they not, I wouldn't be here, talking about it all. I would be at home with my family instead."

She looks at the prosecutor for the first time. Pulls her chair a little closer to the table.

"When the men returned – I mean, when the men came into the house for the second time, was it already dark outside? Was it night?"

"Yes, it was dark. Night-time. The children had already fallen asleep."

"How were you alerted to the men's return?"

"We heard a car pull up. As it swung round, the headlamps lit up the house. One of my aunts said: 'They'll do us all in. Hang us or set us on fire.'"

"Did you hear anyone pray?"

"Yes. My father was a religious man. He always told us to pray to God and ask for his salvation."

"Did you pray, too?"

"Of course I did. But I had been looking around to work out how to save myself. I didn't want to leave everything in God's hands."

"Would you please tell us what happened in the house?"

"That's why I'm here. To tell the truth about my family."

One of the defence lawyers stands up, shakes his head theatrically, and says, "Your Honours ..."

But the presiding judge waves him away and turns to the witness.

"I have to ask you to keep your account limited to what happened inside the house. Anything else will, as you can see, be regarded as provocative."

She nods.

"The door opened and instantly, the flames shot upwards, all different colours, red flames, blue and yellow ones, as if someone had been fanning the fire. I heard screams. The smoke was rising, so I turned my face away and ran to the window. I covered my mouth with one hand and used the other to hit the pane. I don't remember how many times, at some point it broke but only in the same way as windscreens do. It didn't come to bits. Then someone shoved me from behind and I was pushed straight through the pane. My mother shouted, 'Run! Run!' When I turned around, I saw my cousins trying to protect their small children, three children each and they were crying. And I saw my own baby brother and little Emilija, who was only nine. She sat holding her weeping brother on her lap. My mother shouted, 'Run!' But I couldn't. Someone had thrown a hand grenade into the back of the house and shrapnel had struck my neck and head, and one hand – I couldn't feel my body any longer. Then I heard my mother shout once more that I must run. I had fallen but somehow I got up and ran to the stream, where I crouched down to hide. I could see other people jumping out of windows, but the men noticed and shot them."

For the first time, she reaches for the glass of water on her table. She sips, presses the glass against her lips for longer than necessary.

"How many times did you have to hit the window-pane before it broke?"

She puts the glass down.

"A few times, the glass was thick, though I thought it would be thin. Like ordinary glass, I mean. So I hit it quite a few times but I can't tell you how many. I was so terrified."

"How far was it to the stream?"

"Fifty metres. Maybe a hundred. If you'd like to know more precisely ... I don't know. I would really like to go back there just once, to see that house, even more than I'd want to see my parents' house, where I lived for fourteen years."

"Where did you hide after your flight from the house?"

"Under a small bridge. I spent the night there, in the water. While I was under the bridge I couldn't see the house. I could hear the screaming, it went on for an hour or maybe two. The last scream was a woman's."

"You have injuries from that night. Can you describe to us what they are?"

"You only need to look at my hand and my face. What can I say? There was an explosion ... my neck was hit, I was injured all over by the fragments, I had cuts every-where."

The prosecutor puts his papers in an orderly pile and nods to the judge.

While she was bending over him, he started to tug at the zip of her anorak. Seen from above, it might have looked as if she were kissing him. But like her closed eyes, her lips were pressed together. She held his face between her cold hands. When he tried to kiss her, he could sense how she pulled gently away from him, how the pressure from her hands increased to prevent him from coming closer to her lips. He pulled the zip down instead, saw her pale throat with its soft curve and a wide section of her dark T-shirt, far too thin for the time of year. It looks like a river mouth, he thought. Pale skin, flowing down from the neck, spreading under the dark fabric. He loved this delta, would have loved to sink into it. He knew what would be revealed as he pulled the zip down a little more. He knew her body, every part of it, her shoulders where the bones were so easily felt, her wrists which he could circle with his thumb and finger, her small breasts that made him light-headed as he held them, pressed them, kneaded them, clung to them, losing all control, then her belly stretched flat between her hips and with a small navel, little more than a slit, in the middle. So warm was her belly, as though it held a power station within her; its heat surprised him every time. But her toes, her small, slightly crushed-looking toes, were very cold, as if all warmth vanished on the way down her legs; these legs of hers, so thin-looking when she stood naked in front of him, and yet men turned their heads in the street when she walked by in a short skirt. Her shins were blotchy, blue or brown in places, and didn't match the rest of her body. He often wondered about the bruised areas, since he never saw her banging into the edge of the bed or the table legs.

Her eyes were still closed as he examined her pale skin and sensed the soft wind sweeping over her and making her shudder a little. He told her that he had never loved another woman as he loved her. He insisted that he loved every single thing about her and began to list what he meant. Then, on their day by the Baltic Sea, he did not tell her that she seemed utterly untouchable and that, for a moment, he had wondered if ever a man had made love to her, pushed into her body and held her down by her slender wrists. Then, he could not believe that he had done just this. Nor could he understand his desire for her body, a desire that was new to him. Afterwards, seeing how he had left marks on her skin, he would ask himself if he could possibly have caused her pain. This idea came back to alarm him, as he saw her bending over him with her anorak half-opened.

He took her hands in his and looked at her in search of some small irregularity, a blemish, but knew that she had none. She had to straighten up so as not to lose balance. Her fingers were much thinner than his, her neatly cut nails covered with a layer of colourless varnish. He took her hands in his and wanted to warm them. But she could not be warmed. In this, her fingers were like her toes. Whenever he touched her, or she him, these parts of her were always cold. He simply couldn't get used to it. Often, he took her hands in his or made her put them into his pockets or held them against his cheeks or wrapped them around a hot cup of tea.

On that day by the Baltic Sea, he had clasped her hands tightly, as if to squeeze the cold out. He pressed them so hard that she opened her eyes in fright and looked at him. Her face was so close to his and her black hair lifted in the wind, which, he thought, was surely invigorating. "You're hurting me," she said. And he told her that he would do anything to make her happy. "Tell me, how can I make you happy?" But she just looked at him with her large, dark eyes. He knew that if she asked him the same question, he would answer, "Stay with me."

Counsel for the defence rises. He is Mr Nurzet, a man with short, blond hair and strikingly large hands.

"The men who entered the house had robbed all of you and carried out other acts as you have just described them, but afterwards you nonetheless stayed in the house. You were prepared to sleep there, rather than flee. After the thefts, did you not realise the danger? Weren't you frightened?"

She looks down at the tabletop.

"What can I tell you? They took everything from us, leaving only our souls. We didn't think that they would take them away, too. We felt that we were all human beings and that we would learn to live together again. We could never have imagined that they would do what they did."

"Tell me, have I understood you correctly? As a group, you did not leave that house because you believed that no one else would come for you?"

"Yes."

"When the men drove away, did you see the car they used? Did you see the car they came back in?"

"I didn't see the car they arrived in, but I heard it. The exhaust was broken and made a lot of noise."

"And are you sure that it was the same car each time?"

"I don't know if there were other cars. I think it was the same one, but I never saw it, only heard it."

"Can I put it on record that the only evidence for the car the men arrived in being the same as the returning one, is that you believe that you were able to recognise the noise of the exhaust?"

She nods.

"You nod. May I take this as yes?"

"Yes."

"Did you recognise the men who returned at night?"

"No, I didn't. But members of my family said that they were the same men who had robbed us and that they had come back to take our souls."

The expression on Šimić's face – doesn't he look tenser now? Isn't that a smile, fleeting and undisguised? For the first time, he appears to be listening attentively. He no longer plays with his tie or examines his nails, but watches his defence counsel, who stands behind the table, leaning forward a little and sometimes holding himself back as he speaks, as if to control the flow of words.

"When the car returned and brought the men back, was it already night-time?"

"Yes."

"Was the house supplied with electricity? Or were there street lights outside?"

"Lights were on in the neighbouring houses. The electricity in our house had been turned off and there were no street lamps outside."

"In fact, it was dark outside."

"Yes."

It's easy to see what he is driving at. Šimić might well not have been there when the Hasanovićs were burnt alive. The lawyer will argue that his client never knew that the house would be set on fire, and that, after having left with the two men, he had injured his leg, a nasty twist, perhaps a stumble – God knows what happened – and had been taken to the hospital. Šimić knew the truth, but chose to be silent.

He senses the unrest spreading in the public gallery. People no longer appear impassive, instead some are whispering to each other, others flexing fingers or arms, yet others shifting their feet about. It is as if injustice generates tensions which have to find outward expression. There is an itch somewhere inside his body. He can't locate it. He wants to scratch it, but wherever his hand goes, it seems that the source of the irritation lies elsewhere, deeper. His right calf itches, and he tries to get at the spot through the material of his trousers, fails, reaches up under the hem, but realises nothing is any good.

On leaving the room, he hands his headphones to the guard, as required of members of the public. He goes downstairs, across the lobby and then straight outside. For a while, he hesitates on the front steps, then decides to carry on to the gatehouse in front of the court building and get his jacket from the locker. He had to leave it there, along with his identity card. He'll collect them and walk back by the same route he took in the morning – along the Scheveningse Road towards the sea.

It has stopped snowing, but dusk has descended on the town and the first cars he sees have switched their headlights on. How late can it be? He presses his face against the passenger side-window of a parked car, hoping to see a clock among the other dials. He walks on. The pedestrian walkway is covered by a powdery layer of snow which quickly melts under his feet. A woman is walking towards him and he asks her in

English, "Could you please tell me the time?" She glances at him, bunches up the bottom of her jacket sleeve and pulls it back. "Ten past four." He thanks her and sets off again.

She has to endure waiting for another hour. Is a witness allowed just to get up and leave the courtroom? What would happen then? Would she, too, find two guards at her side? But she is there voluntarily, unlike the defendant. Šimić could have come willingly, too. But he didn't. In order to get the trial underway, they had to arrest him and have him transferred him to The Hague. He could at least have volunteered.

He's sweating inside his jacket, even though he's walking slowly. Maybe a tram will come. He turns to look and waits briefly under the shelter at the tram stop. Having a roof so close above his head calms him.

They met in the theatre. She was sitting in the cloakroom at the far end of the wide entrance hall with a mass of coats and jackets behind her. She was absorbed in a book. Her long, slim legs were resting on the counter. He had left the auditorium early and was standing about in the foyer, feeling a little lost. When she noticed him, she closed the book and looked at him. He took a few steps towards her. "Do you like Shakespeare?" she asked, when he came close enough. He wasn't quite sure how to reply and checked the title of the book she had left on the counter: *King Lear*. He could hardly say no. "I adore Shakespeare," she told him. He was taken by the way she rolled her r's, wondered where she came from – was it Poland? Then he learnt that she was a Serb, that her name was Ana and she had come to Berlin to study.

The following morning, he rushed off to a bookshop and bought the Universal Library editions of *King Lear*, *Romeo and Juliet* and *Macbeth*.

If he had he told her the truth, would they have gone out together? He asked himself this many times, because he had lied to her. He had never read anything by

Shakespeare. But he couldn't tell her that on the first evening. It was just a small, white lie, told so that he could be close to her.

> This is the excellent foppery of the world, that, when we are sick in fortune – often the surfeit of our own behaviour – we make guilty of our disasters the sun, the moon, and stars; as if we were villains on necessity; fools by heavenly compulsion; knaves, thieves, and treachers by spherical predominance; drunkards, liars, and adulterers by an enforc'd obedience of planetary influence; and all that we are evil in, by a divine thrusting on.

He stands at the window, his face pressed against the glass. He is looking out. The sky must be overcast, for he sees neither stars nor moon, only a couple of lights in the far distance where he assumes the horizon must be. Over breakfast, he had watched a tanker moving slowly towards Rotterdam across a sea banded by the breaking surf. Now he wonders why there were so few lights – just one or two on that gigantic ship.

When a car corners a bend in the street outside and its headlights briefly sweep the shore, he thinks that he can see the water.

How late is it? Two o'clock? Three? The lounge is dark, apart from the light from a streetlamp on the pavement outside the house. He has picked a small guesthouse. Its name appealed to him and, at this time of year, in December, it was easy to find a vacant room, even one with a view of the sea. It could be that he is the only guest. He has met no one else in the corridor. The house is quiet, no one stirs, and there is no sound of the surf. If he closes his eyes he might be somewhere else, not in The Hague, not in a city anywhere, for urban stillness is different, it has an oppressive quality, like a sluggish substance amassed between the buildings.

That word comes back to his mind: *bonaca*. He looked it up later in a small dictionary that she had given him. He didn't find it.

When the play ended and the public streamed into the foyer, a crowd collected in front of her cloakroom and some people in the queue were waving their numbered tickets in readiness long before it was their turn. Ana took each ticket, went away for a moment and returned to the counter with an armful of coats. She didn't look at the people standing there, only at the numbers as they were presented to her. The cloakroom was hot. Tiny drops of sweat appeared at the top of her nose and, later, on her forehead. When she had taken the last coat off its hook and helped her customer to put it on, she stood still, with her hands on her hips, her sleeves rolled far up her arms. And then he did something that still amazes him today. With his index finger, he traced the ridge of her nose, from tip to bridge. His gesture surprised them both. He was far too unsure of himself, he knew that. He felt certain that, throughout his life, all kinds of opportunities had passed him by because he feared rejection or, worse still, being thought pushy. Ana said nothing.

On every one of the next five evenings, he went to see the play, despite having rather disliked the performance the first time round. Every night, he left just before the interval began, shoving his way past the vexed people on his row in the hope that when he stepped through the door into the foyer, she would be in the cloakroom, just as she had been on that first evening. He knew this wasn't likely, because another woman had taken his coat before each performance and she wasn't like Ana at all.

He didn't know much about Ana – only that she was twenty-seven years old, had learnt German at school in her home town of Belgrade, and later received a scholarship to study German in Berlin, where she had been for a year. At that first meeting, he told her about his father, who came from Karlovac, which pleased her and made her suggest that they should speak to each other in her language. "Sorry, I can't," he said, explaining that not only was he born in Germany and grew up as a German, but also his father had never spoken to him in Croat. "So, you really don't understand a word?" she asked and he shook his head.

She then gave him a goodbye kiss on the cheek, but no phone number where he could reach her and no surname. Only Ana. "Three letters," she said, "it's a palindrome." And there it was again, the rolling r-sound, which stayed with him for days afterwards and which he imitated, or at least tried to, when he was alone. His first name, Robert, had two of her r's.

As he stands at the window, he hears the words in his head once more and speaks them under his breath: Berlin, Belgrade, cloakroom, German – his tongue vibrating lightly against his palate, a puff of air that makes his lips dry – and then his name, as only Ana had pronounced it, until he felt, just for a moment, that he'd heard her speak. Her voice was always so clear, even just after waking in the mornings when he still had to try to clear his own. He often asked her to say something close to his ear and, when she didn't come close enough to tickle him, told her "I didn't hear that," so that her whispering lips touched his ear and, although he tried to hold back, the intimacy of her voice triggered an irresistible excitement. To imagine her whispers now was enough; warmth flowed through his body, down from his throat, through his lungs and deep into his belly. Any old word would have done, but she always made a joke of it and would hiss sentences in his ear that threw him into confusion. "I want you." "Do you like this?" "Shall I?" He feels the thrill spreading through his body.

He keeps standing by the window with his forehead against the cold glass. His jaw is growing numb. His stillness is complete. The room is dark, which is perhaps why he senses her presence so clearly.

Ana is behind him, nearly close enough to touch him, to put her arms around him, to press herself against him. Her breathing, caught by his ear, is the wild rush of air that he's longed for and then, in the stillness after the storm, he waits for the first syllable. Tongue vibrating against the palate, that is how his name begins. A pause before the next puff of air. "You care for me?" Her slender arms around his body. Every day, every night. "Ana, I couldn't hear that." He feels it now, that tickling sensation. But he still cannot hear her. It has now been three weeks and four days. Twenty-five days and nights since he left her flat. Eight months since they lay, side by side, on that Baltic beach. Ten months since the evening in the theatre and the days that followed. And twenty-five days in which his mind has had only one thought: his desire to see her again.

On the sixth evening, she was at the theatre and did not seem surprised to see him. She just took his coat, gave him a numbered ticket and asked him if he was going to see the play. He told her that he had already seen it four times, until just before the interval. She worked only on Saturdays and Sundays, she told him and let him into the cloakroom, though visitors were frowned upon, and they sat there together between the wood-panelled walls, near the radiator, which gurgled to itself from time to time.

They talked about the city. To his amazement, she knew every single nightspot on the Kastanienallee, and on Bergmann Street and Simon-Dach Street. She preferred Lovelite, Maria am Ostbahnhof and a small place called Zosch. He had never been in any clubs. She liked Berlin because it was the kind of city where, whoever you were, there was somewhere for you or, as she put it, a place for you under the sky.

He asked himself where his place might be. He felt most at home in his own small flat and with the other historians in the office where he worked as the assistant to one of the professors.

He imagined Ana among the sweating bodies, a tank top exposing her bare arms and shoulders. She was speaking of freedom and decadence, he of his dissertation. He recalled how once, later, she had tapped him on the forehead with her finger and said: "Life happens outside, not in there."

How had she realised so quickly that the intense wish for what was "outside" was precisely what disturbed his inner balance? He needed someone to provoke him, odd as that might sound. He had felt like this back at school. Come on! Go for it! I dare you! Ana was the first woman who had grasped this from their first meeting. She was the woman he had always hoped for.

Looking back over the ten months, he has come to see that she understood him better than he understood her. And he asks himself if he was too much of a coward. Should he have insisted on answers when her silence and her refusal to tell him more about herself made him feel insecure? He also wondered where it came from, this fear of his that asking too many questions would ruin their love.

There are no more lights out at sea now; the two points of lights from before must have passed out of sight long ago. The sky shows no trace of the advance of the morning.

When he woke, she was lying beside him, her eyes closed, her lips slightly parted, a few strands of hair sticking to her temples. He got up and started to look around her room. During their first few weeks together, he kept trying to decode everything about her. The books she read, the music she listened to, any little thing that might help him to be closer to her, any little thing that might reflect some part of her.

The walls of the room were painted green, her desk was a wooden board on two trestles facing the window, and on that desk next to the computer, there were a pile of papers and a bunch of bright flowers stuck into a vase. He caught himself thinking that there might be someone else. Reality was different from what he had imagined, her rooms were cramped and seemed crowded with special places for objects and shelves full of little mementoes.

The kitchen contained a table and two folding chairs, a fridge that reached up to the shelf on the wall where she kept a few items of crockery. Above the basin in the bathroom, she had lined up a couple of bottles of perfume and some make-up. A pink toothbrush protruded diagonally from a china mug. A mirror on the wall. A small round rug, white on a blue-tiled floor.

That morning was also when he noticed the photograph for the first time. She had hung it on the wall above her desk. It was of a strongly built man with thick, black hair and a broad face. His eyes were her eyes. The small folds on either side of his mouth were instantly recognisable. He was her father. And he had thought him such a warm-hearted father, stern now and then, perhaps prone to anger, but with eyes that spoke of nothing but kindness.

She saw him looking around the room, noted that he stopped in front of her desk and carefully examined the volumes on her bookshelf. "Well?" she enquired and then added, "What have you found out about me?" She pulled the duvet back and patted the mattress gently. When he was lying next to her once more, she hugged him, put her face against his shoulder, and he told her, "I know everything."

He wondered, more than once, if it would have been better for him not to know everything, because this would have left him free to love her without questioning his love. He would never have learnt about all that, had he not wanted to know so much.

He often imagined Ana and himself going to the airport to collect her father. She can hardly wait for the doors to slide back at last and then, among the other passengers, her father steps out, suitcase in hand. She spreads her arms wide, like a small child, only now her father doesn't have to crouch; he only puts the suitcase down and, as she throws her arms around his neck, he places his hand on the back of her head and presses it against his chest. While they hug each other, her father looks around, spots him standing a little bit away and looks him over, without hostility. He doesn't understand when Ana says something to her father. Then her father holds out his hand and says, "Ana told me a lot about you. She is very happy."

The darkness seems to reflect his feelings. How long has he been standing here? Hours? Days? Weeks?

Nothing moves. And he asks himself whether one can be sure that life continues in the dark. Were he not aware of his breathing and heartbeat, no other signs would show that life carries on. The dark is a lake, not a river. Memories come back at night, but at a cost. Once a strangulated cry had woken him and, at the moment of waking, he was uncertain whether he had truly heard it or only dreamt it. He was in her room, Ana lay next to him, she was restless and breathing heavily; when he put his hand on her stomach, her body twitched sharply, but his touch had obviously calmed her, as afterwards she went back into a deep sleep. Had she often been lying at his side, full of anguish, while he failed to notice?

He opens the window. One gust and the cold air takes charge of the room. He lies down on the bed and pulls the duvet up to his chin. The light summery curtains are flapping in the darkness and stirring pages of the newspaper on the table.

He gropes for the lamp on his bedside table, finds the string-pull, puts the light on, throws the duvet back and observes his feet, moves his toes a little. "I like slim men," she once said, "and I like your eyes, you have beautiful hands with slim fingers, I like them and I like your lips. You look good." She lets her fingertips glide over his body, from his forehead down along the ridge of his nose over his lips, over his chin, over his Adam's apple, down in a straight line across the centre of his chest and his belly, lingering with one finger in his navel, avoiding the thicket of hair and moving onto his left leg, onwards across his kneecap all the way to the tip of his big toe; while her fingers were on their journey, he kept his eyes closed and wished he were three, four metres tall.

She used to say that people who don't drink fear life, because the idea of letting themselves go scares them. Then she would light a cigarette. He would think, Such wonderful lips, not too full, not too thin, perfectly curved! They were sitting in her kitchen. On the table, she had placed two glasses and an unlabelled bottle. He could guess what was in it. She explained to him that its name was derived from the Slav word for damson, *šljiva*, and that it came in two shades, pale or golden. To warm up quickly in winter, people heated it with sugar and drank it hot.

"You don't know this? What kind of Croat are you?" She raised her glass and toasted him. "*Živeli*. That's what we say – Let's live."

"Shivily," he said.

She laughed.

This was the only word with a familiar ring to it. He had no idea, though, that it had anything to do with "living". He had thought it just meant "cheers!"

Let's live. Then it was an imperative, but it could also be a plea. Uttered in a different tone of voice or in another situation, that word changes its meaning. He can't help thinking of Šimić and on how, in his presence, this toast would raise a bitter echo. Let us live. He can't help thinking of the television images from Srebrenica, and of Mladić and the Dutch commander drinking a toast together. *Živeli*. And eight thousand people died.

That evening in her kitchen, none of this occurred to him. How hindsight alters meaning and makes even single, utterly harmless words take on other connotations.

Then, he only thought of how good it was to be alive, they drank another toast and another, and he said "*Živeli*" every time.

She laughed, because the alcohol had such a rapid effect on him. "You still have to learn to drink."

"Why do I have to?"

"Because it's part of life."

He closed his eyes as he drained his glass and soon afterwards his whole body felt off-balance. He opened his eyes again and gripped the table with one hand. She watched him, bent towards him, kissed him on the ear and whispered to him in that voice of hers, which he had been in love with for so long, a single word that he'd only known as a name. "*Zlatko.*"

"Do you know what that means?" she asked.

He shook his head.

"Sweetheart."

That word, too, could have such different meanings! He wondered if he and Ana would ever reach a point of mutual trust in the other's language. Sweetheart. How could he ever pronounce that word again? Or hear it spoken?

Next morning, in the courtroom, a man takes his place as a witness. He seems troubled, and clearly doesn't know what to do with his hands, sometimes placing them on his lap, sometimes on the table. He pulls at the collar of his white shirt so often it becomes noticeable. He is gaunt, with sunken cheeks. There is a small piece of plaster stuck on his neck, obviously to cover a razor cut.

The man does not recognise Šimić. He stated that at the start of the interrogation. "No," he said curtly and after a short pause, repeated the single syllable, but this time lengthening it and shaking his head at the same time.

He sits behind the glass, allowing the witness's voice to work on him. He closes his eyes. The man's voice is surprisingly strong; he had expected it to be weaker.

The prosecutor takes his time to look the witness over.

"Could you please tell us what you know about the houses that burnt down?"

"The houses belonged to Muslims."

"How many burnt-out houses do you know about?"

"I can't tell you precisely how many, but I saw several houses on fire. I had a full view of Višegrad from the attic in my house."

"Could you also see the River Drina?"

"Yes. I saw a lot of corpses in the Drina. We couldn't get them out of the water, because of all the shooting. I remember a woman with a small child. They were drifting down the river, sitting on a plank."

"You stayed in Višegrad until when?"

"Until the 14th June 1992."

Mr Bloom pauses, as if to make everyone in the room take note of the date.

"Why did you leave town on just that day?"

"On the 13th of June, a neighbour came to see me. He's a Serb, his name is Antić. He told me that ethnic cleansing would begin soon and that a convoy had been organised to move inhabitants out of the town the following day. He was sure it would be better for me and my family to travel with the convoy."

"Did you trust him?

"Yes, I did. At the time, I thought he was going out of his way to help us. Look, I'd lived next door to him for thirty years. I never had any reason to distrust him."

"Do you know if any official organisations were collaborating?"

"Antić said he had heard on the radio that all inhabitants were advised to leave town with the convoy. The news item had been repeated several times. He also mentioned the Red Cross. But at the time we didn't check up on any of it."

Mr Bloom glances at the presiding judge.

"What happened on the morning of the 14th June 1992?"

"Two buses arrived at seven o'clock. Many of us were waiting. Serbs, too, who had come to say goodbye to us. Some were quite tearful. Then we boarded the buses."

"Did you count the number of people fairly precisely?"

"I didn't count them, but I estimate, say, about a hundred, or a hundred and fifty. Later on, more buses were expected."

"What were the feelings of the people who left on the buses? Were they frightened?"

"We still thought that we'd be saved. We trusted the organisers."

"And the Red Cross?"

"There was no Red Cross to be seen."

Yesterday, a woman testified to meeting Šimić on the bridge and how he had offered to take care of her family; the image has stayed in his mind: Šimić just standing there, alone on the central part of the bridge. In his imagination, the man looks lost, abandoned. He has tried to give him the face on the other side of the glass screen, but all the time he sees the man in the photograph, the man with the warm, kind eyes.

"Who came with you?"

"My wife and my two daughters."

"How old were your daughters at the time?"

"One of them, Ivanka, was fourteen, and her sister Branka was nine."

"Did you stay together on the bus all the time?"

"No, the buses stopped quite soon after we'd left Višegrad. Women, old people and children were all taken to the other bus and the men came onto ours. The other bus drove on, but ours turned and went back in the direction we'd come from. The bus stopped again a little later and we spent the night in a forest parking area. It was dark and we had no lights."

"How many men were there on the bus?"

"I reckoned forty, but many were lying down in the gangway and I'm not sure I counted everyone."

"What happened next?"

"A car arrived in the morning and a couple of men climbed out; they were armed, and they came onto the bus and ordered us to hand over everything we had. Documents, watches, jewellery, money. They had a bag sent round for us to put our things in."

"What was the ethnic origin of the men already on the bus?"

"Muslims, one hundred per cent."

"Then what happened?"

"They tied us up, with our hands behind our backs. They used cables. Then we had to get out of the bus, one by one. We had to kneel alongside each other. I was the last in the row."

Throughout, the man has seemed distraught, but now he is suddenly at peace, his hands rest on the table and his fingers are still. It is hard to endure this sudden calm. Even the interpreter seems to notice. Somehow, her voice sounds a fraction quieter.

"Please continue."

"One of the men asked me how many Serbs I had killed. None, I said. That wasn't what he wanted to hear, he told me. Then I felt a blow at the back of my neck."

"At the time, what went through your mind?"

"It's difficult to put into words what went through my mind. My brain had stopped working, somehow. I couldn't think clearly. I looked around and noticed that some of the men were missing from the row. Then I saw the Serbs pulling the next lot into the forest. In an instant, I ran. At first I heard nothing, then someone shouted. And then the shooting started, shots all over the place, really wild. I don't know what happened behind me, but I suppose the others had started running, too, trying to escape, and that's what saved me, because if I had been the only one, one of the men could have run after me and caught me. All I wanted was simply to run as far and as fast as I could. I slipped down an embankment, got up and ran across a road. And ran on, until I reached a village where I felt safe."

"What happened to your family?"

"My family was all right. The bus had taken them to Skopje. But a week went by before I heard about that."

"Have you found it difficult to speak about this in court?"

The man put one hand over the other. For first time, he looked around the courtroom and acted as if he wanted to quickly observe each of those present, starting with the prosecutor, then the judges, the defence lawyers and, finally, Šimić.

"I am here because no one must forget what went on. Memories will be kept alive for as long as there are people who tell their stories. And the hope is that remembering will lead to the guilty being punished.

Staying silent helps them. That's why it's not difficult for me to sit here and tell you what happened."

Ana let him have her volume of *King Lear* in English. It was bound in dark blue cloth and the first few pages were only partly hanging on to the strip of glue. He wondered how often she had opened the book, how often her fingers had leafed through the pages. On the second page, he found a handwritten dedication. Two blue-ink sentences in Cyrillic script. He could only read the date: 10.4.92. Ana was eleven years old in 1992.

When he asked her about the dedication, she replied that her father had written it. He wanted to know what it said. "For my Cordana," she told him. "He wrote that I should always have this book at hand, because no one knew more about life than Shakespeare." She remember-ed the words by heart, didn't even have to glance at the book. He took it in his hands. Then he opened the cover, turned the page and pointed to the word before the date. "What does it say here?" She glanced at the page and said, "Višegrad." He wanted to know if it was a town, and she said it was a small one in eastern Bosnia. It made him wonder. "I thought you came from Belgrade?" And she answered, "We lived in Višegrad before." She said nothing more after that, but he said, "Cordana. I like that name."

At home, he later tried to find the town whose name he had never heard before. He examined photographs on the Internet and learnt of its famous bridge, built at the time of Ottoman rule and central to the novel *Bridge over the Drina*, one of the volumes in Ivo Andrić's Bosnian trilogy. In 1961, Andrić was awarded the Nobel Prize for literature.

He also learnt that the town became tragically famous as the second Srebrenica in the last Balkan war. He read about the corpses in the Drina and about the people of Slap who, on a spring day of 1992, dragged the first dead bodies out of the water and, though they were strangers, buried them in the nearby cemetery. And how, over the next few weeks, the river washed up hundreds of bodies. By then, the people in Slap knew they had to bury the corpses in secret. To avoid attracting the attention of Serb snipers, fifty-odd neighbourhood volunteers carried the dead to their graves during the dark, still nights. They buried one hundred and eighty bodies; later investigations showed that of all the corpses pushed into the Drina, only one in every twenty was hauled out of the water. Between April 1992 and October 1994, thousands of Muslims from the Višegrad area were either terrorised or killed. While reading up on all this, he tried to imagine Ana in the small town where people were slitting each other's throats. He tried to imagine her standing on the bridge, leaning over the balustrade and looking down on the Drina. But instead of the corpses, he saw only the sun glittering on the rippled surface of the water.

Ten years passed before two suspected perpetrators were arrested and transferred to The Hague. Milan Marić and Boris Lukić. They were charged with being responsible for the death of one hundred and forty individuals. At the time, Marić was twenty-four. People remembered the young Serb as a good neighbour before the war, someone who had Muslim friends and would now and then go with them to the mosque. When the war started, he styled himself "Avenger" and began a career of torture, rape and murder.

This was also the first time he heard of the crime of locking forty-two members of a family into a house and setting it on fire. Marić, Lukić and their accomplices were again thought to be the perpetrators.

He wanted to take Ana in his arms, comfort her and look at her, push strands of hair away from her face. He wished she would tell him everything, because he thought it would help her. Talking, it's the only thing left to her, he thought.

He read Andrić's novel and developed an affinity for the River Drina, even though he has never seen it. He almost longed for the river, a greenish, foaming body of water that flowed through gorges and valleys within its steeply rising banks. It was her childhood river. Every day, as she stood on the bridge and looked up the river, she saw the tall, dark mountains that ringed her town.

The water was green, greener than anywhere else, and teeming with Danube salmon. Shoals of big fish would shelter in the shade under the arches of the bridge. Andrić writes about the Black Man, who lives in the middle pier of the bridge. Inside the pier is a large, dark room. If the Man shows himself, whoever sees him must die. The middle pier had a large gap in it, like a huge arrow slit. From the riverbank, the children would stare into the hole, as if into an abyss. Trembling with curiosity and fear, they would watch the wide, inscrutable opening, until something seemed to move inside, as if a black curtain had twitched. The first one to see it had to call out. At night, many children struggled with the Black Man of the Bridge, as if with grim fate, until their mothers woke them and drove their terrors away.

When she slept badly at night, he put his hand on her belly. Perhaps he should have made her wake up. Perhaps he could have comforted her.

But what did he know about war? He had grown up in a small German town. His childhood passed in a place where hedges were trimmed, lawns mowed and Sundays spent quietly. People fought, but only behind closed doors, and when a neighbour called to borrow the lawn-edging power tool, the grown-ups chatted about the poor summer weather and the state of the garden and the new people in the house down the road. Like so many other young men, his father had gone to Germany to find work. He had got himself a job as a car electrician and then fallen in love with a German woman. He married her a little later. Two of his brothers had gone to France and only their eldest sister still lived in Karlovac.

He was fourteen at the time war broke out in Ana's country. He wasn't really interested, and when his friends looked to him for explanations of why the war had begun and whose fault it was, he knew himself to be as ignorant as they were. When people asked him about his religion, which was often, his usual reply was that his family was Catholic, although it hardly seemed worth mentioning, since faith had so little meaning for any of his relatives. One of his aunts stayed on in Karlovac throughout the war and it was said that the town was under heavy attack, but even this wasn't often talked about at home.

He watched the television news and saw people running in the streets of Sarajevo, heard the shooting and wondered if it was for real, because it sounded so different in films. He saw some people left lying in the street until others came along, hauled them into a car and drove off at speed with the doors hanging open. He saw clouds of smoke rising towards the hilltops and, up there, the large artillery barrels rotating. He saw sobbing children who clung to their mothers' skirts and emaciated men behind barbed-wire fences. In one sequence, soldiers were toasting each other before it cut to weeping women. He watched a bridge collapse on itself and a priest sprinkling a tank with holy water. All these images stayed in his memory and yet there were other things that mattered more to him.

He could never have told her anything about this. He could not admit to her that no one had spoken about the war at school, or that friends of his parents had moaned about how the war had stopped their holiday trips to Yugoslavia's Adriatic coast. When they spoke of how often they had gone there, what a lovely time they used to have and how nice the people were, he had heard his mother say, "It's too, too bad" and leave it at that, though what she had meant was unclear. His father had said, "They've all gone crazy down there." How could he tell Ana of this massive indifference?

He wanted to show Ana that he was not indifferent – not to her, nor to what she had experienced. He set about reading books and articles about the war with a will. And he never missed an opportunity to take Ana in his arms and hold her tight.

Hardly a day went past without him seeing Ana. Most of the time, he slept at her place and went from there to the university. He lost contact with his friends. He wanted to be with her whenever he had a chance. Often, he would wait for her outside the door to her seminar room or outside the front door to her apartment block, if she wasn't in when he called. Sometimes one of the people who shared her stairway would let him in and then he would sit on the step opposite the door to her flat, intrigued that so many people could pass the nameplate next to her doorbell without any idea of the wonderful woman who lived behind that door. Every time he pressed the bell next to her name, his heart was in his mouth. He liked her surname, because, like her first name, it was a palindrome, or almost. Only the last letter disturbed the harmony, that "c", which is pronounced "itch". Šimić. Like her first name, her surname suited her. Both had a pleasing symmetry about them.

Every day, he longed to see her again. And she felt just the same. When he waited for her at the university, she sometimes played a trick on him. She would pretend not to recognise him, walk straight past and then whirl about, put her arms around his neck and press her lips to his ear, saying, "There you are, at last."

He had read once that happiness differed from normality by three to five heartbeats a minute – as if it were so easy to prove: simply place a couple of fingers on a pulse and count. Five extra beats define the condition of happiness. But she was made differently. He felt sure that her heart beat more slowly, maybe five to ten beats less per minute, when she was near him and at peace. At first, he used to joke about it and put it down to his soporific aura, until he realised that no one else had been able to give her what she longed for: a feeling of calmness. She called it "anaesthesia". She often wanted it. When she leaned against his chest and soon dozed off, he took pleasure in his good fortune.

His friends said that they barely recognised him, that he had somehow stepped out of his usual self, like a jacket worn inside out. They wanted to meet the woman who had caused the change. Her name was Ana. Ana, with one "n". She was a Serb, he explained. "A Serb?" And he would say "Yes", and reflect on what Ana had told him about this. At some point, she had started to deny her nationality. Now, if someone asked where she came from, she would reply "Slovenia", because she was fed up with the question and didn't want to talk about the war, or anything to do with Karadžić, Mladić and the rest of them.

When their relationship was in its fourth week, his best friend invited them for an evening meal to celebrate the end of his trial period as university lecturer. He asked five other friends, moved the kitchen table to the sitting room, covered it with a white sheet and surrounded it with all the chairs he owned.

At first, they spoke about work and mutual friends. Ana couldn't really join in and he wasn't sure that she was enjoying herself. He tried to pull her into the conversation by telling everyone that, during the vacation, she had worked as an intern at a market research company, but stopped after two weeks because all she did was check newspaper articles and make coffee. One of the guests asked her what she would like to do once her studies were finished. And Ana replied that she wasn't sure yet and that, at first, she would probably have to return to Belgrade.

Belgrade was a trigger. "Have you seen the photos of Karadžić?" asked his friend's girlfriend. "I never thought they'd get him in the end. A faith healer! Honestly, you don't get more cynical than that."

He saw Ana briefly close her eyes.

Someone wanted to know how a man like Karadžić could possibly live in peace in Belgrade, travel by bus, give lectures on alternative medicine and have a favourite corner bar where, once in a while, he would play folksongs on the one-string fiddle. A false name, a pair of glasses, a long white beard and his hair tied back in a pigtail had clearly added up to complete camouflage. He looked like a Pope in the photographs. "The entire world was chasing after him and, all the time, he was doling out business cards with his mobile phone number on them! It's unbelievable!" exclaimed one of the guests. "He seems to have been quite a hero to the Serbs," said another guest. "There were street protests after he was arrested and people turned out in their hundreds, even the politicians."

He had of course followed the newscasts, too. When he read about the case in the paper, he excitedly phoned Ana to ask if she had heard the news. "Yes, I have," she said. "Didn't you live in Novi Beograd?" he asked her. "Yes," she said. "Me and half a million other people." It had been a short conversation, which left him with the impression that he was more excited about the capture of Karadžić than she was. He couldn't understand why she had seemed so indifferent on the phone. She might have said "At last!" or, even "Thank God!" But that night, when they were in bed together watching the news on TV, she didn't say another word, so he told himself he'd better not ask her anything more about it. Instead, he pulled her a little closer.

"It's interesting," said the girlfriend of one of the guests. "I mean, I'd like to know what kind of people turn out in the streets to support a mass murderer." While she spoke, her eyes were fixed on Ana. He asked if there was any more wine and wanted to know where his friend had bought the wine, because it really was good. But it didn't work. "Aren't you pleased that they've got him now?" asked the man who was sitting next to Ana. She put her glass down. She took so long to reply that the circle of friends around the table stilled and went quiet. "You believe that it's all over now," she said. "But it's not over. And it won't be over even when they tick the last name off their list."

When they walked home together, he asked her what she had meant, but she told him that she'd said enough for today.

The third witness states that Višegrad was never so clean as it was during the months of war. The people looked after their town. Normal waste collections stopped, of course, but ordinary people took over all the jobs. Everyone cleaned the pavement outside his or her own house or business, and teams of citizens were formed to tidy up in front of public places like the post office, the banks and the parks. Cleaning up became quite popular and before long the town had improved beyond recognition. Every day, between nine and ten in the morning, they all turned out to tidy the place up.

The small, plump, round-faced man informs the court of this good citizenship and goes on to point out that his own neighbourhood had been especially filthy, because it had been the area worst affected by the flood of muddy water from the dam. Broken tree trunks and branches were scattered everywhere, but they cleared it all up.

And they had Zlatko Šimić to thank for this. He was the one who persuaded people that something had to be done and organised the street cleaning. On the first day, men drove around the town in a car with a loudspeaker. The message was that everyone was to meet up and then, in front of them all, Šimić put forward the idea of cleaning the town. People trusted him; he was a university professor after all. They knew him and were happy to be given a task. Everyone could see the results. It was quite the talk of the town. For one thing, many of the shop windows had been broken and the pavements were covered with broken glass. The shops had been owned by Muslims and since most of them were not around any more, no one had tidied up.

The witness is one of Šimić's neighbours. He looks rather lost standing there in his oversized suit and tie. He is clearly trying hard not to say something wrong. His first response to each question is a brief pause, and he often looks at Šimić before speaking.

Mr Bloom, the public prosecutor, rises to examine the witness.

"Do you believe that the Muslims who helped you clean up were afraid?"

A few moments of complete quiet.

"I don't understand what you mean. Afraid? Afraid of what?"

"You have just told us that several of the Muslim-owned shops had been abandoned. We have heard other witnesses assert that everyone knew of Muslims being killed and that it was also well known that houses belonging to Muslims had been set on fire. Would you agree that the Muslims who were still in the town might have been afraid?"

He looks at Šimić and then at Mr Bloom.

"Yes, of course I would. It's natural that anyone who has seen a neighbour's house burn or maybe a person being killed or raped would be afraid. Anyone would be scared in a situation like that. I was frightened myself."

"But you have suggested that Muslims willingly helped you to clean up."

"That's not the same thing. It's a different kind of feeling, when you worry about your house looking tidy and when you fear for the future. What I mean is, they're two separate things. Cleaning up around your house is one thing and thinking about how they might come for you in the night and kill you or take you away, well, that's another."

"What you're saying, in other words, is that people who fear being killed during the night might also worry about the cleanliness of their home?"

"People always like their place to look good, surely."

Silently, Mr Bloom looks around the room, as if he wanted to make sure that everyone in the room has taken this sentence on board.

"I have one more question. Is it true that Herr Šimić in his role as ... let's call him 'commander' of a small army of cleaners, wore a red ribbon around his right upper arm?"

"As far as I remember, yes."

"Please describe this ribbon"

"It was tied around his arm. It was broad and made from a kind of red cloth."

"In your view, might some people have taken this ribbon to be the sign of the Red Cross?"

"I don't think so. There was no cross on it."

"Thank you."

She told him that she couldn't understand why he took so little interest in his origins. "Your family comes from Karlovac, there is Slav blood in your veins and you have a Slav surname, but you can't speak the language and know nothing about our country. Why do you deny it? All that is part of you, isn't it?"

He didn't know why Ana had been struck by this on that particular day; perhaps it was because he hadn't known anything about a famous Serb singer called Ceca and had displayed such amazement at the music she listened to, a kind of folk pop called Turbo-Folk. She even knew the lyrics and sang along while she washed dishes in the kitchen or sorted the pile of clothes in her room. For him it was as weird as someone of her age humming along to German popular songs from a bygone era.

"I don't deny that it's part of me," he said. "It's just that I've never really been in close contact with the culture. It's hard when you don't speak the language."

"Why don't you just learn it, then?"

He had often been asked that question. Every time he would say well, yes, perhaps he should try to learn Serbo-Croat, but he never did, because it pained him even to think of picking up a new language. At school, he had found French and English hard going. His father, who after forty years still sounded like a foreigner, had always insisted that his son speak German to avoid the problems he had encountered.

His father was always utterly certain that his own future was in Germany and never entertained the idea of going back to where he'd come from. He found nothing attractive about the country he'd been born in and his family had always lived in. The son could never remember his old man listening to Yugoslav music or buying a Yugoslav newspaper, and only heard him use his old language on the phone to one of his sisters.

"I would learn it for your sake," he said.

"If you don't want to learn it for yourself," she insisted, "you mustn't do it to please me. All I want is to understand why you feel the way you do."

"It's probably true that I was never very interested in the Slav part of me."

Would things have been different if he had spoken her language? Would they have trusted each other in another way, would their relationship have changed?

One evening, Ana cooked for him. She made the stuffed cabbage dish called Sarma. "It's my father's favourite," she said.

It was the first time he saw Ana wearing an apron. Now and then, she consulted a notebook she had placed on the table. Ana's grandmother had used it to write down her recipes. The book had been handed down to Ana's mother on her wedding day. "This notebook was one of the few things my mother took with her when we left Višegrad," Ana told him. He leafed through the pages, as if he could read her memories in it.

Often, if he felt like a distraction, he would play a game which entailed choosing what he should take with him if he had less than a day to leave town for ever. He'd take documents, obviously: things like a passport, a birth certificate and formal references. Some clothes; he never cared much for clothes and the choices seemed easy. Books; now, that was hard. *Homo Faber*, *I'm Not Stiller* – would that be enough? *The Discovery of Heaven*, but that was a volume of some eight hundred pages and the hardback copy was very heavy. What would he do about the notes for his thesis? With them alone his suitcase would be bursting. Did he have any mementoes? Nothing came to mind except for a small stone Ana had given him, a pebble from the Drina. Perhaps some photographs. A couple of CDs. In his mind he would then run through his CD and book collections, ranking the items in an order that changed every time he thought about it. And he wondered how hard it would be for him to leave all the rest of his belongings behind. Surely it would be like losing a part of his life? Worst of all, for him, would be not knowing what would happen next; so he felt the only way to cope when you suddenly have to flee is to avoid thinking about either the present or what lies ahead. But surely that would be impossible.

Ana put the large stew-pot on the table and pulled her apron off. "The real skill is not to leave bits of string in it," she said. She watched as he lifted a forkful to his mouth. The flavours hit his tongue, the slightly sour chopped meat mixed with raisins and rice inside the cabbage wrapping. It tasted of going visiting as a child.

His father loved that dish and his aunt had cooked Sarma every time they went to see her. As a child, he would listlessly poke about in the stuffing. He didn't tell Ana that he still disliked the acidic bite of the cabbage.

He no longer hears the courtroom arguments; instead he sees himself and Ana sitting at the table while she flattened cabbage leaves to be stuffed, and he thinks that he might after all belong to her life. Ana might have actually regarded him as a member of her family or, at least, she might have imagined it.

Her grandmother must have followed this recipe when she cooked for Ana's grandfather, so did her mother, cooking for her father and, now, Ana for him. Was this a sign? She missed her family, she said, and told him how they all used to sit around the table together, her father and mother, her grandparents and her cousins.

She simply couldn't understand people in Berlin, because no one she had met of her own age felt particularly sad to be away from family life, from parents, brothers and sisters, grandparents. Everyone seemed to prefer getting as far away as possible. Where she came from, things were different. Her grandparents' house was next door, her uncle and aunt lived nearby and she walked to school with her cousins. She often wondered why people here were so accustomed to being alone.

Ever since that evening, he has wished he could join her family circle. He sensed that she might be someone different there, happier among those who knew who she was and spoke her language. He asked her when she had last been home. She told him: the day she fled the town. "Why haven't you been back?" "Because I want to keep my memories," she said. "The lovely memories of my childhood."

They sat at her kitchen table with their empty plates in front of them. He thought of the small photo on the windowsill of his parents' bedroom, a framed, sepia image showing his family, all of them gathered around a table in the garden that belonged to his grandparents. Granny and Grandad had been alive at the time, and the brothers had brought their families to see them. Staring at the camera, the family sat on wooden benches around a table covered with a white plastic sheet and laid with plates, glasses and bottles. He was there, perched on one of his grandfather's knees, while a little girl, one of the cousins he thought, sat on the other. Strange, how this photo seemed familiar and alien at the same time. There he was with his immediate family, but now he is unable to even put a name to all those faces.

> Many a time he danc'd thee on his knee,
> Sung thee asleep, his loving breast thy pillow
> Many a story hath he told to thee,
> And bid thee bear his pretty tales in mind
> And talk of them when he was dead and gone.

Ana, why didn't you talk to me about the burden you carried? I have asked myself that so often during these past weeks and now I do it again, alone in a foreign hotel room which you could be sharing with me. You could have told me everything. We sat in your kitchen and waited for the tea to brew in our cups. I thought it was just that you needed more time. But even when the tea was ready, we continued to sit in silence.

It was the morning after that night in the park, which you must surely remember as I do. Often during the past two weeks, as I've lain here thinking, I've wondered if you too have been stretched out on a bed somewhere, searching in your mind for images of us and our shared memories. I wonder if we conjure up the same events or if you see different ones, or the same ones from a different perspective, maybe in different colours. I imagine being you. Imagine your kitchen and you, seated with your back towards the window, the same place every morning, because you chose to sit there on the first day, and it became our rule for your small table. My chair would be opposite yours, so I faced the window and its view of the grey wall of the house next door. I prepared mugs of tea for both of us and put them on the table. After a while, I would pull the tea bag from your mug, wrap it around a fork and squeeze it dry. This always amused you, just like my way of scraping the last drops of yoghurt from the carton. You joked about these things. You thought it must be something about the Germans, to do with wartime deprivation, a folk memory that passed from one generation to the next, from grandparents to parents and on to their children, and so inevitably to my children, because I'd end up giving them the same example. You said, "Your children" and although it wasn't an issue between us, we simply hadn't got that far, I felt a little peeved all the same, because you could have said, "Our children."

As we sat at your table that morning, you knew what I was waiting for – that I wanted to hear from you how things stood. You saw it. You sensed it from the way I didn't say so. It was hard for me to understand what images from the previous day had stayed with you.

Mine are ever present. The two of us, wandering across the meadow in the Pleasure Garden by the River Spree. The blue sky. Later, on the river bank, we stood close together. You with one foot on the lower bar of the railings. Pleasure steamers chugged past. You told me about Belgrade and its fortress, where you loved spending the summer evenings looking down at the view of the River Sava flowing into the Danube. "Oh, look! Do you see that little boy?" you exclaimed. "Over there, with blond hair and a cap," and you pointed him out to me. The little boy sat between his parents on the seat right at the back of one of the steamers. His father was a large, heavily built man, his mother held out a mug in one hand and a half-eaten roll in the other. You waved and shouted until the boy looked your way. He kept looking at you until the boat was out of sight.

I felt as light as a balloon and had to hang on to the railing to stop myself from rising into the air and floating away. You had picked that little boy out from all the other people on the boats. And I wondered if you knew that I was that boy, that my mother had offered her child the roll with salami and my father had stared into the distance, as if none of it had anything to do with him. And I said, "I love you."

And you turned around and kissed me. "*Moj zlatko*," you said.

For the rest of the day, I felt released, outside myself, as if a burden had been lifted from me and I had rediscovered some childlike state of safety and happiness. Perhaps that was why I played hide-and-seek in the park that evening. I like it when dusk creeps over the landscape and makes the flowers fade into shadows;

there is something exciting, something unreal about night-time in the woods. For me, it has always felt like another and contrary world, so unlike the cosiness of indoors. As darkness fell and we strolled together, I led you through the park, away from the paths, among and under the trees. The leaves on their stilled branches were not so dense that we could not catch glimpses of an unfamiliar sky and I felt the same thrill that used to come over my schoolboy self during those nocturnal escapades, when we sneaked out late from where we boarded at the summer camp and wandered off into the forest, armed with torches and full of scary stories, the braver boys a little ahead, the less brave behind, sticking close to one other. To hide behind a tree and then leap out screaming was simply what one did.

Ana, I didn't give it much thought; I just slipped away, hid behind a tree, sneaked up behind you and jumped on you, wrapping my arms about you as I did. In the past, girls had always taken fright and yelled, but calmed down soon enough, insisting that it wasn't funny in the slightest. Afterwards, they had quickly forgotten the whole thing.

But you were different, you screamed and your body wouldn't stop shaking for a long time. You burst into tears and when I tried to take you in my arms, you fought to get free until you realised that the arms around you were mine and you let me hold you. I was dismayed by how heavy your soft body had become. That night, the light in the hallway was left on and I understood that the reason was not that you'd forgotten to turn it off. You wanted the light on and I let it stay on, long after you'd fallen asleep. That night, I lay awake for what seemed like hours, thinking about what might have happened to you in Višegrad.

But in the kitchen the next morning, you still didn't want to speak about it. Now, I've come to believe that you were unable to do so. Your silence had already lasted far too long. I was absorbed by the sight of your toes, once you kicked off your girlish pink felt slippers, stretched out your foot and made your toes wander up my leg. As your foot climbed higher and you slid closer to the edge of your chair, your toes almost reached my belly and then clamped themselves onto the top of my thigh.

You made me laugh when you showed me your toes for the first time, those small, wrinkled toes you didn't like the look of. When you climbed out of the bath and walked barefoot across the tiles, you would always notice that I was staring at your feet and hurry into bed to hide them away under the duvet. And when I dived face first under the cover and worked my way down to kiss your feet, you defended yourself by pressing one foot against the other. You told me I should kiss any part of you but not your tiny, hateful toes.

He sits at a table in the guesthouse conservatory and looks out over the restless sea. He can see white horses far into the distance. A couple of joggers are struggling against the gusts that sweep the promenade. From where he sits, they seem to be running on the spot. Nothing else suggests the strength of the wind: no litter flying in the streets, no creaking woodwork, no whistling and whining noises.

There is something utterly unreal about the world outside. He visualises Ana down there, by the sea. She is wearing an anorak he doesn't think he's seen before. The hood is pulled over her head, and she stands waving to him with her back to the sea. Why doesn't she sit next to him here? The table is laid for two. Opposite him there is a place set with an empty plate, a folded napkin next to it, a knife, a fork and a cup. But Ana is out there.

Perhaps she simply woke early and, while he still slept, went over to the window and saw the sea. So she dressed, pulled the door shut behind her and ran towards the seashore, and whenever she comes back to the guesthouse, he will be there, on his seat behind the windowpanes of the conservatory.

He imagines her running towards him and, when she reaches his table, pulling back her hood to reveal her ruffled hair. She bends over him, and her lips and cheeks are very cold. He watches her as she pours herself a cup of tea and butters a roll. He asks her if she has slept all right and recalls how they fall asleep, one body against the other.

When he arrived late at night three days ago, the woman in reception let him have a double room for the price of a single, so it had two of everything, two duvets, two pillows, two large towels, two small face towels and two soaps. He tried to imagine which side of the bed Ana would have preferred, which towel she would have taken if she had been the first to run a bath, and which of the two small soaps she would have unwrapped. Every morning he has woken up in this place, he has found his head resting on her pillow.

They were in bed together when he asked her. He was lying on his back and directed his question at the ceiling. He waited until she switched off her bedside light. Gently, he asked why she had left Višegrad, back then.

The sound of her voice surprised him, it was different, so soft and vulnerable.

"My father wanted us to leave," she said. "He didn't want us to stay. He sent us to Belgrade to live with his sister."

"Why didn't he come with you?"

He could hear Ana breathe. He placed his hand on her belly.

"He didn't want to go. Didn't want to leave our house."

As he went on questioning her, his voice seemed to escape his control and he needed to work hard to modulate it.

"Ana..." he began and paused. "Ana?"

He noticed that her regular breathing was interrupted for a moment and the surface of her belly did not rise; at that moment he too held his breath.

"What happened in Višegrad?"

He no longer recognised his own voice. It was like hearing a recording of it, and once more he felt he couldn't connect to it. He sensed that her belly once more rose and fell to its old rhythm.

"They shot at the town," she said and her voice was clear again, at least clearer than before. "There was a war on. Many fled."

"I've never known," he said, "anyone else of my own age who has experienced war, who has had to flee in wartime. In this country, fleeing was something our older people had to do."

She straightened up, leaned against the wall and pushed his hand away.

"I often ask myself where we would be without the war. Would outsiders, strangers, even know where Bosnia is on the map if it hadn't been for Gavrilo Princip and that war? I often feel that war defines all of us – Serbs, Croats and Bosnians. Who did what? Who has experienced what and where? Where does the guilt lie? Given the same time and place, I could easily have been born a Bosnian. I would be the same woman, but you would see me differently, because you would perceive me as a victim. But because I'm a Serb, everyone thinks of me as a potential culprit, even though they know nothing about my life. And meantime they all forget that there were victims among the perpetrators and that some of

71

the victims would have turned into perpetrators, given half a chance."

She pauses for a moment.

"You couldn't know, but I'm in Berlin because of a grant they gave me as a descendant of a victim of the Nazis during the Second World War. My grandmother was held in Jasenovac, the largest of the Holocaust camps in the Balkans, and was deported to Leipzig where she was assigned to a forced labour squad in a hotel. Of course I thought about all that before coming to Germany. But it never occurred to me to get involved with the history of the German people, even after I met you. I wanted to know more about your background, because I hoped to understand you better. Everyone seems to think you can't mention Serbia without saying something about the Battle of Kosovo. But who cares? It happened more than six hundred years ago. What are these wars to us? When they shot at my home town, I was eleven years old. And you weren't even born when the Nazis were killing millions of people. Your grandfather might've been one of them – I don't know. Or maybe he helped Jews to hide. I've no idea. Whatever he did, it's got nothing to do with you."

He was astonished at where this conversation was leading. He had wanted to know about her life, back in the town where she had grown up and which she had left so abruptly. He had wanted to know what she had gone through because he sensed that she was still living with it. But she was giving the whole thing a political dimension, which seemed unfair and wrong in their situation, alone with each other and together in bed. Above all, it wasn't justified, given the reason for his question, which was that he cared for her very much. The vehemence of her argument made him angry.

"Now you're making things hard for us," he said. "Of course your views would be affected if you were to find out my grandfather was a Nazi. Your grandmother was held in a concentration camp – surely you can't tell me it wouldn't matter one bit if you were shacked up with the grandson of a Nazi?"

"Come on, you can't inherit guilt. You can still be a wonderful human being, even if your father killed someone. Maybe just because of it, you'd do all you could to be different. My grandmother never talked to me about what happened to her during the war, but my mother did. What if I had never heard any of it? My knowing couldn't have been important to my granny, otherwise she would have said something. She didn't, not even when I started learning German at school. So, in your opinion, was it my duty to ask her? To push her into telling me things she'd rather not speak about? What's the result of someone not knowing anything about particular events in the past, or of not wanting to know or not wanting other people to know? Would that person's development follow a different path? Would life change for any of the people around him? Or wouldn't both that person and the others feel less encumbered, less inhibited in their life together? I often think so."

He refrained from contradicting her, from arguing that human history is all about cause and effect. One thing follows from another. It is impossible to simply excise a chapter from history. No war comes out of a void; there is always a prehistory. When tension mounts, it can somehow create an atmosphere conducive to making certain ways of thinking and behaving acceptable to the majority. Historians have observed that wars start during such periods, that the origins of war can be understood only in terms of historical processes.

But he didn't want to start this kind of talk with Ana. To him, the idea that the Balkan war could come between them seemed absurd, although he was aware that German bombs, too, had been dropped on Belgrade. He was unsure about the justice of bombing the Serbs. After all, the NATO attack on Serbia was driven by Germany's guilty conscience, its historic culpability. The German Minister for Foreign Affairs said he had learnt a lesson: no more Auschwitzes. And so bombs rained down on the city where Ana lived with her family and friends. What was their connection to Auschwitz?

He could find no peace after that conversation with Ana. He felt her behaviour had been emotional and unfair, and he agonised over this for days. He had once lunched at the university canteen with one of his professors, who knew a great deal about Balkan history, and asked him if he thought that the Serbs, like the Germans, carried a burden of guilt. The professor looked up at him quickly, put down his fork which had already speared a piece of meat, and wanted to know if his questioner had ever heard of the SANU Memorandum.

"You see," he said, "it was the Serbian Academy of Sciences and Arts that provided the ideological framework for the idea of Greater Serbia."

This was the first time he'd heard of the memorandum.

"Well, what would your view of it be?" the professor went on. "Given that it was a paper published by a group of scientists and academics, which demanded an end to discrimination against the Serbian people, discussed whether Serbs should commit genocide against the Albanian population in Kosovo and argued in propagandistic terms for the national and cultural unity of all Serbs, regardless of which region or federal republic they lived in. This paper was debated in public for five years before the outbreak of the war and was incorporated into the government's political program. What do you think – is this a case of unshakeable resolve? Or of emotional imbalance? I tell you, the murder of Muslims was planned. In my opinion, people were, in general, willing perpetrators. Haven't you seen the images showing the first tanks rolling towards Croatia? The citizens were lining the streets, waving and throwing flowers at the soldiers."

He didn't know what to say. Why did he ask about the Serbs' guilt? He didn't tell the professor anything about Ana. Following that conversation, it became clear to him just how subjective the matter of guilt can be. Had the professor's explanations turned out differently, he would have told him that he was in love with a Serb woman, who questioned her share of the guilt. He treated Ana as someone defined by her nationality. It made him feel ashamed. Is it not true that ultimately guilt is a sick feeling and a psychogenic delusion, and that to burden oneself with the past is the symptom of an illness, whereas healthy people look towards the future?

"Why bother with the sea if you can't go for a swim in it?" Ana asked.

The question returns to him unbidden as he stands on the beach at Scheveningen. He left the guesthouse after breakfast, with a desire to be by the sea, to feel the wind and to hear the surf. Above all, he wanted to be out of that conservatory. It's chilly, like the early April day he and Ana spent by the Baltic Sea. Most of the cabins and seaside cafés are boarded up. A couple of dogs are chasing each other; their masters keep their distance, each to his own, hoods pulled low over their faces.

He was barely outside the guesthouse door before a gust of wind tugged at him so hard it almost took his breath away. He walks along the promenade for a bit, and stops where he has a view of the open sea on the far side.

Back then, by the Baltic, he asked himself if the water would continue flowing onwards through all the seas. If the water, which the force of the waves sent crashing up the beach, would later turn up along the coasts of other countries. It occurs to him that this thought was like the red dot he had put on a currency note when he was a child, in the hope that it would one day be returned to him. Could it be that the water he's looking at now has come here from the Adriatic Sea?

At the Baltic seaside, he recalls, he pulled off his shoes and socks, and rolled his jeans up to his knees. The cold gripped his feet in an instant, but he still attempted to breathe calmly, took one step out into the water, then one more until he stood with both his feet up to the ankles in seawater. He closed his eyes. His blood pumped rhythmically through the arteries in his neck; he had to force himself not to gasp for air. He felt the cold creeping high up into his legs and in under his jeans. He curled up his toes in the sand and they sank in deeper with every wave. He thought of the Adriatic, of the warm, alluring Adriatic, flowing in gentle eddies around his legs. He heard the distant cries of children struggling for possession of a lilo, the spluttering engine of a fishing boat, then a woman calling, a voice he knew well. After-wards she laughed as he tried to warm his feet, first by rubbing them with his hands and then trying to push his feet between her legs, which was a struggle, as she was pressing her thighs together as hard as she could. He had come dashing along from the sea, full of glee, run around her a few times and then allowed himself to collapse on the sand, crying, "Hey, who says you can't bathe in the sea."

The last time he'd been on the Adriatic coast was as a child, more than twenty years earlier. He could hardly remember anything of where he'd gone with his parents, or where they'd stayed. The only image that remained in his mind was that of an old colour photograph of a pebbly beach, his grandfather sitting on a deckchair, his mother stretched out on a towel and himself, naked and holding a fishing net, silhouetted against a deep-blue sea.

He knew that Ana and her parents used to go to the Adriatic every summer and always stayed in a place called Lumbarda. Ever since she'd told him that, he'd wanted them to go there together. "Let's go," he said. "Then you can show me what you used to do on your holidays." "Maybe we will, one day," she replied. That was where the matter ended.

He thinks about this now, as he stands watching the waves which, for the first time since his arrival in The Hague, have white, foaming crests. Perhaps he should ask her just one more time. Summer will come again and it might be good for her, good for both of them, to go together to an untroubled place from her childhood, back to somewhere free from ghosts of the more recent past. After all that had happened in the last few weeks, he would dearly like to go there with her.

She must feel, he thinks, that Lumbarda is somewhere from another time, uncontaminated by what would happen later and free from thoughts of war, guilt and crime. Surely she can have only happy memories of that bay with its small offshore islands, as he has seen it in a travel guide – a bay in which the sea, a solid blue mass of water, lies so still like that its peace will never be broken by winds and currents. But was it really possible to keep these memories apart from all that has happened since? Memory can be fatally impaired by a single event, which casts its shadow over everything and drives away all peace of mind.

Ana fell in love for the first time in Lumbarda; she was ten years old at the time and the object of her desires already a young man, an actor from Sarajevo. She told him this story when the two of them were playing spinning-the-bottle. They did this sitting opposite each other on bare floorboards in her room with an empty wine bottle between them. He had to spin it several time before the neck of the bottle pointed towards her. She could choose between action and truth, and she chose the truth. He asked her who her first love was.

"Macbeth," she said.

The young man had recited *Macbeth*, perched on a cliff by a small inlet. She'd watched, listened as his voice rose above the sounds of the sea and seen him check the book he held in his hand, when unsure of his lines.

In a deep voice, accompanied by sweeping gestures, she mimicked him:

"Who can be wise, amazed, temperate and furious,
Loyal and neutral, in a moment? No man:
The expedition of my violent love
Outran the pauser, reason."

And she laughed because, in retrospect, it was so obvious that she would fall for the first man who could recite Shakespeare. Did her father read Shakespeare aloud to her when she was little? "To my father, Shakespeare was life."

He wanted to know what had happened in this, her first affair of the heart, and she said the end was tragic. She continued with her story, which amused her greatly, of how her father, once he had realised what an impression this actor had made on his daughter, had ordered him to stop acting in front of the girl. And then, when her Macbeth asked her father who he was, her father had replied, "Titus Andronicus."

To her, this was a mere anecdote, a moment of paternal craziness, which demonstrated how much he cared for her and to which she clearly attached no deeper meaning. And to him, too, it came across as a burlesque scene featuring an eccentric father. It was only later that he looked back and tried to extract from this story an early insight into her father's inscrutable character. A man who called himself Andronicus – wouldn't that carry some weight with his prosecutor? Members of the Court, consider that the man who stands before you had named himself after the most brutal avenger ever created by Shakespeare. Might it not be evidence of an evil streak which, long before his crime, had lain undisturbed deep inside him and only surfaced when the rules of civilisation were set aside and replaced by the anarchy of war?

After listening to her anecdote, he decided to read that most miserable of Roman tragedies: fourteen murders, culminating with Andronicus arranging a meal for the Emperor's wife, at which she is served the flesh of her own sons. To say "I am Titus Andronicus", was this not an attempt to be something more than a mere onlooker? Was it not a frank expression of his desire for greatness, the ability to fashion a tragedy with such an impact that it would condemn not only himself to ruin, but also others. Surely such thoughts must have occurred to Ana, too?

You told me of your Sundays together. Sunday was when you and your father would go for a walk along the banks of the Drina. You always ran along after him, trying to keep up with his long strides by stepping on the same tussocks and patches of gravel. You watched his rucksack as it bounced up and down, making the tackle rattle a little. You sat next to him while he fished and kept an eye on every twitch of the float. And when it started to dance about furiously and disappear under water, you were so excited and keenly observed your father's calm movements as he played the fish, each time pulling it in a little closer. You waited for the moment when the fish would finally emerge from the water, fly wriggling through the air and land with a splash on the stones. Then he would hold it firmly against the ground with his fingers inserted into its gills until the tail and fins stopped flapping. To please him, you tried to kill a fish, but couldn't bring yourself to do it. Although you realised that a fish must be killed before it is eaten, you couldn't rid yourself of the vague sensation that there was an alien side to your father, that for a moment he had turned into another man, as if you had caught sight of him in a distorting mirror.

Wasn't that how you felt? I did. Surely you remember me telling you of when I found two puppies dumped in a wood? They were whimpering softly and huddled together inside a cardboard box. One puppy had a cute black spot around one of his eyes. I carried them home and intended, first of all, to give them something to drink, and then buy them dog food and find a blanket to cover the box. My plan was to put the box next to my bed. As I was walking along, I speculated about what to call the puppies, but when I got home and went into the kitchen to look for a small dish, I heard my father say to my mother, "We can't keep dogs. Dogs are a pain in the neck." He filled a plastic bucket with water and held the puppies under until they were both dead. All the time, I stood in the doorway and simply couldn't take my eyes off him. Even now, this image is sharp in my mind. The ground seemed to have suddenly split open, allowing me to look down into an abyss, into a dark rift. I'm not sure if this was the reason why I could never again bear to drink from his glass.

I clearly remember you raising the white mug to your mouth, the mug with a small chip off it – it's absurd to recall the chip, but I do, perhaps because at the time I worried about the sharp edges of the crack catching and cutting the lips I loved so much. You held the mug with both hands while I asked you about your relationship with your father. You stared at me in disbelief, or so it seemed to me, at the suggestion that one could have a bad relationship with one's father. "I love my father," you said, with just a hint of incomprehension. And perhaps you also felt it was a challenge, I'm not sure, as if I had doubted your love for him. But what reason would I have to doubt?

Do you know what I thought the first time I saw his photograph? I thought that you were lucky to have a father like him. And that you must have many good memories of this man. I liked him in that photo, with his slightly sceptical look, though there was nothing cold or distant about him. The scepticism, I felt, hid a kindness that made him always ready to reach out to his fellow men.

When you hung the photo next to your desk, it was enough to convince me that he meant something special to you. It wouldn't have occurred to me to put my father's picture on the wall, even if he were dead and the image held a particular memory. But your father wasn't dead. Or possibly he was, even though he lived.

That was when I got this idea in my head. Perhaps he was lost to you, in another way, that's true – but nonetheless, a sense of loss drove you to put his likeness on the wall.

You've told me how it amazes you that I discuss my father so coolly, that any son could speak of his father in that way. I tried to explain that I had always wanted him to show some weakness – even something like breaking his ankle when he went hiking. And that I even used to wish I'd been hurt in a car accident he'd caused. I dreamed of how, standing by my bedside, he would be forced to admit his guilt, since he'd been in the driving seat. I grew up in his shadow and lacked the strength to move out of it.

He was so full of life, always loud and always strong. As I've told you, he used to call me *zeko*; for a long time I didn't realise that the word meant "little rabbit". He liked to tell me stories about his early years in Germany, how he started out with empty pockets and went on to make something of his life, how he would often stay late in the garage to work on the cars to give me a better life than his own.

One of his workmates once knocked into a jack and released the safety catch when my father was lying underneath. Everyone expected to find him dead. He said that the doctors couldn't get their heads round the fact that all his internal organs were undamaged and that they had to let him go after just an hour in the hospital. Another of his stories was from his boyhood in the Pioneers, when he was sent off to spread tarmac on the coastal road during a summer holiday in Dalmatia. He was already apprenticed at the age of fourteen and had a trade at sixteen, while I was still sitting at a school desk at eighteen.

I did not tell you that whenever there was something to celebrate, especially within the family, he drank too much and started shouting at my mother; once we even went outside to sleep in the woods until he sobered up. I have often thought that this is why I don't care much for alcohol and why I'm unenthusiastic about the prospect of family holidays. And I also wonder whether my father is the reason why I never learnt his language and have resisted, consciously or not, everything else to do with his share of my origins.

Even if one's father has been a constant source of irritation, it seems that, for reasons I cannot comprehend, his voice will echo in one's mind well into old age. My relationship with my father is still far from good, but all the same – or perhaps precisely because of that – I cling to the good memories that always exist when you long for them so much.

I never forget the time we played football in the garden, just because we fancied it at the time, and both of us stumbled at the same time and ended up side by side on the lawn. To this day, whenever I think of that afternoon, I hear the sound of his heavy breathing, and to this day, I can sense the happiness of the seconds spent lying next to him on the grass.

Mr Nurzet, Counsel for the Defence, rose to speak, but first looked quickly at his colleague to the right. She acknowledged his glance with a brief nod.

"Zlatko Šimić was born into a poor, honest farming family. He learnt independence early. He helped his parents on the farm and looked after the cows and the pigs. Generally, he was very fond of animals. He once brought up two piglets and pleaded tearfully for their lives until his father weakened. He loved to go riding. Ever since his earliest years, it made him happy to sit astride a horse. He was his father's pride and joy. Zlatko Šimić was the first in his family to attend a secondary school and he went on to study English at the University of Sarajevo. Later, he became a professor at the same university and an internationally recognised expert on Shakespeare. He started a family, saw his two children grow up in a house he had built for them. He never had any conflicts with Muslims.

"His life changed in 1988. That was the year he lost his beloved son. The boy was sixteen when he died in a skiing accident in Slovenia. They spent two days searching for him. He had frozen to death when they found him. I believe that every one of you can imagine what losing a son must mean to a father. Even today – and this event took place twenty years ago – I honestly believe that you will respond to the pain you can still see in his eyes. That was when he started to drink. There were a few hospital admissions and he occasionally underwent psychotherapy. You will hear witnesses confirm that Zlatko Šimić was sometimes so drunk that he would hold himself responsible for the tragedy.

"Since the death of his son, Zlatko Šimić has been a broken man. As you get to know him better, you will realise how unimaginable it is that this man, who appears before you, would have committed the crime you have heard him charged with in this court. It is true that he was in Pionirska Street on the day of the 14th of June 1992. He happened to be walking along the street in the direction of the town centre, when a group of women, children and elderly people were moving into the House by the Stream. He was also about in the street in the afternoon, but at quite a distance from the house in question. Walking past, he had spotted a horse in an abandoned yard. He went to get the horse and later rode it through the centre of Višegrad. It had rained that day and the streets were slippery, which may or may not have been the reason why the horse fell. Zlatko broke his shinbone in the fall.

"There were witnesses present and you will hear them describe what happened. One of them called the ambulance and Zlatko was taken to the hospital in Višegrad. A doctor examined him and referred him to the hospital in Užice for an X-ray of his leg. They took Zlatko to Užice by ambulance, but broke the journey in Vard-ište, a place on the road to Užice, where Zlatko's cousin owned a café. They stayed in the café for a while.

Because of the cold, Zlatko was given a blanket. He remained in the ambulance all the time. They continued the journey and reached the hospital around ten o'clock in the evening. It was already getting dark.

"Zlatko Šimić could not have participated in the murder of the women, children and old folk. He didn't even know of the fire that killed the Hasanović family during the night of the 14th of June 1992. Zlatko Šimić cannot even comprehend that there are people capable of doing something so dreadful."

The defendant seems to be moved by his counsel's words. While the lawyer speaks, Šimić is once more sitting up straight, breathing deeply and occasionally scratching his nose with his index finger. He closes his eyes, letting his chin rest on his chest, and, as his head tilts forward, a lock of hair slips out of place, strays down his temple and ends up hanging in a narrow fringe over his forehead. He makes no attempt to tidy his hair or get his comb out.

As the trial progresses, he gradually loses the conceit that he knows what's going on. Perhaps this is all part of the tactics adopted by the defence.

He asks himself if he was right to return to The Hague. But he wanted to be there when the defendant took the witness stand, wanted to hear the man's voice and find out how Šimić would defend himself against the prosecution's arguments. Of course, he couldn't have stayed on in The Hague for weeks on end and had to return to Berlin by the end of the first week. He assumed that his own impression of the man would be formed by then, but the first two days were enough to prove him wrong. He was quite unable to detach Šimić, the man, from the place where he observed him and from the accusations against him, even though he has a right to be considered innocent until proven guilty. It seemed likely that the dozens of witnesses and experts, as well as an incredibly large mass of evidence, meant that a whole year could pass before the court reached its decision.

Why has he returned? Perhaps because to him, Šimić is the Black Man of the bridge over the Drina, and he can't stop himself from staring into the dark slit. He is obsessed by the thought that he might have something in common with Šimić. He can't work out what it is and wishes that he could simply get the man out of his mind. They both love Ana. What does Šimić know about him? he asks himself. What has Ana told him? He knows that she has been writing to her father. Has she sent him a photo?

He fears that Šimić might recognise him, pick him out among the members of the public. Look straight at him and smile.

When the counsel for the defence has finished speaking and sits down, the presiding judge addresses him.

"You have indicated that X-ray images were taken in the hospital. However, no X-rays have been included in the list of evidence presented to the court. They could be very important."

The lawyer rises once more and, as he stands, strokes the folds of his robe with his right hand. "Your Honour, I agree that the X-rays would have been very important evidence. We would have greatly preferred to present them to the court. However, in Yugoslavia, the practice was to hand over the films to the patient and, unfortunately, the defendant no longer has them in his possession. When he had to leave his home, he could only manage to take a few things with him. The X-rays were not among them, because he assumed that he would never need them again. However, Mr Šimić will state that such films existed."

The judge gestures towards Šimić.

"Very well, Mr Šimić, would you please take the witness stand now?"

Why did Ana never tell him that she once had a brother? He has learnt about him here for the first time. Clearly, he was her older sibling: in 1988, she was seven and he sixteen. What reason did she have for keeping quiet about her brother?

His mind is in a whirl. A brother who froze to death after a skiing accident. Ana. Where was she while all this happened? Why doesn't the defence ask where Ana was at the time?

Early on, he asked her if she had any brothers or sisters, but she only shook her head and he had simply accepted that, like him, she was an only child. Now he feels betrayed. She has kept many things from him, that much has become clear. Actually, he has been aware of this throughout the months he has known her, but he had no idea what it was she was so secretive about: her father's crimes, the death of her brother. What will be revealed next?

Mr Nurzet catches Šimić's eye and nods almost encouragingly.

"First of all, Mr Šimić, I would like to ask you a few personal questions. You were born in Višegrad, am I correct?"

"Yes."

"What is the name of your father?"

"Ranko."

"And of your mother?"

"Ana."

"Your date of birth?"

"I was born on the 25th of August 1948."

"Do you have any sisters or brothers?"

"Yes, I do. Two brothers and one sister."

"When did you start your own family, Mr Šimić?"

"I married in February 1970."

"When were your children born?"

"My first child, a daughter, was … in fact, my first child was a son, but he died at birth, in 1970. Then my second son arrived on the 10th of June 1972. He died in an accident in 1988. Our daughter was born in 1980. In other words, I have one daughter and I thank God for her."

His counsel nods.

Šimić rests his hands on the table, right hand on top of the left. He sits with his almost straightened arms stretched out in front of him.

"Where was your place of work?"

"I held the chair of English at the University of Sarajevo."

"Have you been involved in any conflicts caused by ethnicity?"

"No. I always had good relationships with everyone. At the university, we worked together as colleagues and no one ever asked what the other person was – Croat, Muslim or Serb. It was of no interest."

For the first time, Šimić raises his head and meets his lawyer's eyes.

"Mr Šimić, we will now go on to talk about your health. You suffered some injuries – injuries and fractures. I am right in saying, am I not, that on the 14th of June 1992, a riding accident caused you to break your leg?"

"That's correct."

"Had you ever broken your leg prior to this?"

"No, neither an arm nor a leg. Not even a finger."

"And after 1992?"

"I broke the same leg again in 1994."

"In which hospitals did you receive treatment?"

"On both occasions I was admitted to the hospital in Užice."

"Have you been an in-patient at any other point in time?"

"I was treated for a lymph gland condition in 1976. I spent two months in the Pod Hrastovima hospital in Sarajevo. In 1989, I was in hospital care because of my problems with alcohol. I was treated at the neuro-psychiatry unit three times, I think."

"Would it be correct to say that, prior to 1992, alcoholism was the reason for you being hospitalised?"

Silence for a moment, then the interpreter's voice over the headphones: "Your reply was inaudible."

The presiding judge intervenes and asks the defence advocate to repeat the question. Mr Nurzet clears his throat before turning to Šimić once more.

"Mr Šimić, I ask you this for a second time. Prior to 1992, were you hospitalised because of your alcoholism?"

"I said that I was in hospital for the first time in 1976 because I needed treatment for my lymph glands, but afterwards, yes, I confirm that I was in hospital twice because of my alcohol dependence."

"Can you describe how it affected you? Did drinking make you aggressive?"

"No."

"I will be more specific. Did you ever become physically aggressive?"

"No."

"Have you ever attacked another person?"

90

"No, never. I have never attacked or injured anyone."

"Were you in Pionirska Street on the day in 1992 when you suffered an injury?"

Silence once more. And once more, the presiding judge has to remind the witness, "The interpreter didn't hear your reply, Mr Šimić. Yet again, you seem to have lost your voice. You must keep in mind that we should all be able to hear you and that includes the interpreter."

Šimić nods.

"Yes. I was in Pionirska Street on that day."

They were together on the bed, she sat between his legs and he leant his back against the wall with her head on his chin. They often read the same book sitting like this. Over time, they had become used to a shared reading speed and often managed to turn the page at exactly the right moment. Her knees were lightly bent, next to her on the floor she kept a glass of red wine. Now and then, she would reach for it and drink without looking up from the book.

It was one of those evenings when they hardly talked at all. He was pleased when they just read together in this trusting way. But for him, unlike her, reading was never quite enough. Distracted by her presence, he would look up from the lines of text to gaze at her legs, the way they were angled and her slender ankles. At home, she would put on her black-framed glasses, which he liked because they made her look so different and earnest. He told himself that he was the only one who saw her face like that; surely it meant that he belonged in her life and that they shared a togetherness that went beyond falling in love and experiencing that compelling curiosity about each other.

Once, she put the book down, got up, walked over to the bookshelf to pull out a cardboard box and carried it back to the bed, where she settled down with crossed legs and the box in front of her. She put the lid down close by and took out a bundle of photographs. She then examined one photo after the other, handing them on to him in turn. She said, "You're always so keen to find out what the place I come from looks like." When he had scrutinised the first few photos, she moved closer to him and explained to him what they showed, often pointing with her finger and every time touching the image.

"My mother in our garden. We always used to grow tomatoes in the summer. Did you know that our word for tomatoes is *paradajz*?"

It was one of the few words that stuck in his mind, because it sounded like "paradise".

"That's the old bridge. When the weather was fine, my father would often sit on the stone seat in the middle. Look over there. He could sit on that seat for hours, alone or in the company of friends. His horse, look. I'm not sure where he got it from. My mother said that he was very happy with the horse. He would spend time with it every day, feed it and groom it. Look, this is the house where we lived." It was a large house, three stories high and built of red brick which on the top floor was not covered with plaster. A vine was climbing up one of the walls.

It was the first time he had seen pictures of her part of the world. An almost idyllic peace emanated from the photographs.

Now, looking back, he knows what was missing in her box. There was no boy in any of the photos, no boy who looked like her and could have been her brother.

Once again, he listens to the voice of the defence counsel.

"Mr Šimić, I would like to find out what you remember of that day and especially of the time you spent in Pionirska Street."

"Frankly, I only learnt here in The Hague that I stand accused of a crime in Pionirska Street."

"We will get to that point. Can you remember what you were wearing at the time? Did you carry anything in your hands?"

"I had put on a sweater and a pair of corduroy trousers. The sweater was a dark shade. I think it was black."

"Did you have anything on your head?"

"I don't know. I simply can't remember."

"Did you hold anything in your hands?"

"No. Nothing I remember anyway."

"What was your destination that day?"

"I was going to Vucina."

"Did you meet anyone?"

"Yes, a friend of mine. A man called Mujo. He's from Sase and came past my house daily on his way to work."

"Did you have a chat with him?"

"Yes."

"About what?"

"I asked him something like 'What's new?' He replied, 'Nothing. Well, we've got to leave.' I wanted to know why. I still recall him telling me that his wife had already left the village. He offered me his cows. What he said was, 'I own two cows, would you like to have them?' I said, 'Mujo, what am I supposed to do with your cows? I don't need cattle.' I told him not to worry, that all this madness would soon pass. Look, the whole thing happened sixteen years ago, I can't remember whatever else we talked about at the time."

"Were other people present?"

"I do remember him saying that they had to be off. There were other people around at the time, women as well as men. I remember the weather. It was overcast and very windy."

"Did you speak to any of the others?"

"No."

"Before you met Mujo, were you aware that a group of people had to leave Višegrad?"

"No. I had heard nothing about that. I had no idea that anyone had to leave Koritnik. And I didn't know either who or what the reason was. No idea. If I hadn't met Mujo, I would simply have moved on. What I'm trying to say is, I had no previous knowledge about these people. That the Red Cross had sent them along to Pionirska Street and so on."

"How did you know about the role of the Red Cross?"

"Mujo told me."

"Mr Šimić, have you ever worked for the Red Cross?"

"No."

"Have you ever pretended to be a Red Cross worker?"

"No. Why should I?"

"At your encounter with Mujo, did he ask you to write anything down for him?"

"No. Why should I have written anything for him?"

"Did you have paper and pencil on your person?"

"No."

"Once you said goodbye, did you go to collect a horse?"

"Yes."

"Did you see Mujo again on the way back?"

"No. As far as I can remember, I didn't see anyone. I was on horseback and when I was about to leave the town, it started to rain. A brief but heavy shower."

"How fast did you ride?"

"Not fast at all."

"And then you took a tumble?"

"As I passed a restaurant, I heard somebody call my name. It was Professor Mitrović and I tried to turn back. In that instant, the horse fell and pulled me down with it. The horse got up almost at once. I tried to stand, but found that I couldn't. Professor Mitrović felt my leg and told me he thought it was broken. He called the ambulance and it arrived in ten minutes, perhaps fifteen. I was taken to the hospital and X-rayed. The doctor said that I had broken two bones. He bandaged my leg and sent me on to the hospital in Užice."

"Did they take more X-rays there?"

"Yes, they examined my leg. A doctor Jovicić confirmed that it was broken."

He would often look at the photograph in the morning, while she was still asleep. He always woke before she did. He made coffee and brought her a cup in bed or, if he thought she was still fast asleep, ambled over to the window to look at the sky or study the photo which was the only picture she had put on the wall above her desk.

It seemed to him that this Titus Andronicus was keeping an eye on her. There were days when the man's gaze seemed sterner than usual. He would conduct internal dialogues with him, calling him Titus. This made her father smile. So, she has told you? It's an old story, you know. She was ten years old. He imagined her father pouring him a glass of wine: they sit together at the wooden table behind the house, with their backs resting against the wall as they enjoy the shade and the view of the garden where Ana is stretched out under a tree, lying on her front and propped up on her elbows to read a book. Her mother brings a plate of tomatoes, places a knife across the plate and a small salt cellar on the table. Before going back inside, she too takes a moment to look at her daughter. Ana's father pushes a glass towards him. *Živeli.* Drink to Life. Ana glances at them. Later she will tell him how pleased she is that he and her father are getting on so well. "He has taken to you. You're like a son to him."

Was that what he wanted? That Šimić would accept him as his son? At the time, he couldn't have known how inappropriate this fantasy was, since he didn't know that Šimić had had a son.

"Have you been awake for long?" Ana asked. She was suddenly standing behind him, holding her cup of coffee.

"Do you think your father and I would like each other?" he enquired.

"Why do you ask?"

"I'm not sure. Or rather, it's simply because I see his photograph every morning. I keep wondering if he'd like me."

"I think he would."

"But you're not sure?"

"He would like you."

"What about me? Would I like him?"

"I can't think of anyone who doesn't like my father," she told him.

He could not help thinking about his own father and wondering if Ana would like him. Very likely she would. Some of his friends were very enthusiastic about his father. He was the only one who felt something wasn't right. His old man was liked because he was entertaining and always ready with yet another anecdote. Once, after being introduced to his father, one of his female friends remarked that he seemed so gentle, such a truly sensitive person. He couldn't help thinking that their acquaintance had been far too brief for her to make that judgement.

He conjured up an image of them both, Ana and his father, talking animatedly, excluding him and laughing together at the dinner table in his parents' house. He would feel jealous rather than pleased. Later, his father would go on about how attractive she was and that he hoped his son realised how lucky he was. And as he walked her home, she would say how strange it was that the two of them were father and son, given how very different they were.

His father knew about Ana, he had phoned and told him about her. "Good, good," his father had said, "I hope this is serious." He had gone on to explain where Ana came from and that she was a Serb, but his father hadn't commented in any way.

Šimić's posture doesn't change as he stands in front of the judges with drooping shoulders and restless hands. As if he doesn't know what to do with his hands, he first puts one on top of the other as if in prayer, and then adjusts this pose almost immediately.

"Mr Šimić, how long did you have to stay in hospital?"

"I should explain that the doctor needed to make a small incision into my heel and attached a couple of weights to my leg in order to stretch my muscles and let the bones knit properly. Or, at least, that's how the operation was explained to me. Whatever the reason, when I came round from the anaesthetic, I was in bed in a hospital ward. And I had to stay put for three weeks."

"Is that to say that you were confined to your bed for twenty-one days?"

"Yes, it does. I was unable to get out of bed."

"Did you know how many other patients were in your ward?"

"There were four of us. My bed was by the window. An old man from Užice was next, then a Muslim from Gorazde, they had amputated one of his legs, and finally another man from Užice."

"Did you spend three weeks in the orthopaedic department?"

"Yes."

"And after that?"

"I was admitted to the neuropsychiatric unit. The unit was part of the same hospital, but housed in another building."

"Why were you transferred?"

"I was in a difficult, emotional state – moody and unbalanced. I was anxious and saw visions. I imagined all kinds of things, saw myself speaking with God and the Devil. Satan's eyes were like two full moons. He had thousands of noses and great long horns, ridged and furrowed like the surface of the sea. My head was constantly full of strange images I couldn't rid myself of."

"Thank you, Mr Šimić."

He is sitting behind the plate glass, staring at Šimić and reflecting with some relief that Ana clearly takes after her mother, at least in appearance. Her cheekbones, pale skin and dark hair offer him at least the possibility of imagining that she is not Šimić's daughter. How often over the last few weeks has he wished that her father were someone else, that the man in the dock were not a blood relation of hers? But he knows that Šimić is her father. He knew this for certain from the first day, when the man was escorted from the adjacent room. He recognised her eyes, her serious, dark eyes in which he had so often lost himself.

In his dream, Šimić enters his room. He can't see his face, only the outline of his body. There's no light to see him by, but he knows it's Šimić. He tries to make himself see, to recognise the things in his room by their shades of darkness.

Šimić moves purposefully, as though he knows the room. He skirts around the two chairs at the table and walks straight over to the minibar. He immediately finds the handle and opens it. The carpet is lit by the dull light from the fridge. Šimić pulls out a miniature bottle. He settles down at the table with his legs resting on the other chair. He unties his shoelaces, leans back, stretches his arms above his head and yawns.

Later, Šimić is sleeping next to him. He tries to turn the light on, presses the switch, but nothing happens; he wants to get out of bed and struggles with the duvet. It ensnares him and however hard he tries, he cannot free himself. Šimić pulls him close and puts a hand over his face.

It's the middle of the night. He gets up and gropes his way through the dark to the bathroom, where he pushes the mat in front of the basin with his foot to have something to stand on. He holds his hands under the rushing water from the cold tap.

The mirror reflects only darkness. Once back in the room, he cautiously opens the fridge to check that nothing is missing.

Ana knew from the start that he doesn't drink. And she was right that he was afraid of letting himself go. Perhaps afraid of life itself. He grabs a small bottle at random. Unscrews the top and drinks the contents in one go, without knowing what it is. It burns his throat. "*Živeli*", she said. And "*Živeli*", he repeats.

Then he goes back to bed.

"What's your problem, lad?" It's Šimić who asks him this. He's still there, at the table, with his legs resting on the other chair. "You know, sitting stiffly in the courtroom all day, that's not for me. Anyway, what do they want of me? They don't know me. All these people so busy sitting in judgement over me – it's crazy, don't you think? They should be asking you the questions. I mean to say, you're the one who knows me – right?" He fetches another miniature from the fridge, drinks it standing up and breaks the empty against the wall. "I loved him. As God is my witness, I loved him. I would've loved you. Clearly, I'm fated to lose my sons."

"I saw myself speaking with God and the Devil."

Those words, more than any others, never leave him in peace. Why did Šimić say that? To order his confused thoughts? What had been plaguing him, what had been tugging him this way and that between two extreme moral positions? Were his actions a burden on his conscience? When Šimić spoke of dialogues with the Devil and his witches, was this yet another sign of his own tragedy? Or was it Shakespeare? Perhaps Šimić was broken and mentally disturbed – or did he only imagine all this in retrospect?

The judge had to tell him twice to sit down, because Šimić just stood there, seemingly unaware of where he was. "Mr Šimić, please sit down." As far as Šimić was concerned, this was a voice from another world and it didn't quite reach him.

Where had his thoughts drifted? Did he recall that image of the bridge? Or a vision of the people who had been relying upon him, all in one long line – the old folk, the women and the children? People who had wanted nothing more than to leave the town, to get out, regardless. Did he dread their faces? Did they haunt him, night after night? You couldn't live with yourself afterwards. Could you ever be free of all these faces?

There was nobody there to hold him, take his hand and whisper his name. Zlatko, you are here because they were hungry and you did not feed them. They were thirsty and you gave them nothing to drink. They were strangers and you did not invite them in. And now the highest court has sentenced you, and you will be punished for eternity.

Šimić didn't defend himself. He didn't teeter. He didn't collapse. "Mr Šimić! Please sit down." He sat down. Then he turned towards the public. He looked at them, all those faces behind the glass, one by one. But his eyes never met anyone's.

He had spoken to Ana about the court. They had even argued about it for a while. At breakfast time, he had seen it mentioned in the newspaper and read the piece out to her. Vojislav Šešelj, charged with very serious war crimes, had gone on hunger strike and now the court was doing all it could to keep him well enough for trial.

"So what? Why read it aloud?" she asked.

"I don't know," he said. "I thought it might interest you."

But why should it interest her? Because it had something to do with the war? Because the accused was a Serb?

"Do you want to know what I make of it?" She pushed her cup away and looked straight at him. "I can understand him," she said. "The court is prejudiced against him. It has nothing to do with justice."

At first, he couldn't work out if she was serious or said it to provoke him. He still isn't sure. She was in an edgy mood. She might have expected him to start speaking about the court and was ready to release the tension that had built up inside her. It was obvious that the court was on her mind. At the time, he had no idea of just how much that particular court of law mattered to her. But he sensed her anger.

"How can you tell?" he asked.

"If it were true that the court is as unbiased as everyone says, they would've put Clinton and Schröder on trial and all the other western politicians as well. Everyone who was responsible for bombing a sovereign state. Which is what Serbia was, you know."

He said nothing.

"Do you realise what it was like? No, how could you know? You've never experienced bombs falling on your home town. It's not like on television."

This sounded like an accusation. It wasn't his fault, but he felt complicit. How could she blame him for observing the war from afar? Did this mean that he wasn't competent to speak about it? "I'll never forget when it began," she said. "I was in the cinema. The film kept running as if nothing was happening. But when I went outside, I saw that the sky was red. Red with fire, because the bombs had hit the oil refinery in Pančevo, which is some twenty kilometres from Belgrade. People were running in the street, but I just stood there. I didn't know what was going on. I just watched people and the cars jamming the street. I spent the night in a metro station, together with lots of other people, and went back home in the morning. Later on, I didn't leave the flat for days on end. Friends came and we sat around talking and watching the telly whenever the power was on. At one point I had to sit an oral exam. The professor was questioning me while the air raid sirens were blaring. Three months of terror, but no one has been held accountable. Do you think that is right?"

What could he say to her? Yes, I think it is? For the first time, she had told him what it had been like for her when they bombed Belgrade. And what about him? He felt hurt. Hurt, because she had excluded him, because she insinuated that he couldn't engage with her past and denied him any capacity for empathy.

Hadn't he tried to understand her right from the start? Hadn't he read books to get a grasp of her history? Hadn't he endlessly reflected on his own history and, because of her, felt ashamed at being so ignorant of his origins? He had thought of his aunt, who lived in Karlovac and of how little concern he had felt for her fate when the war broke out in Yugoslavia and the mortars began to hammer the town. The war had just begun when his father phoned his sister to ask her if she would like to come and live with them in Germany. His mother didn't think much of this idea and his parents rowed about it. Who knows how long this war will last, his mother argued, for all we know your sister might be stuck here with us for months, maybe even years. He, too, felt uneasy, because his aunt would have had the use of one of his two tiny rooms. His father said that when all was said and done, she was his sister and if she wanted to stay with them, they had to take her in. Then brother and sister talked briefly on the phone and when his father put the receiver down, he said: "She doesn't want to. She'd rather stay where she is. 'If a bomb hits me it's meant for me. That's life,' she says." His mother was visibly relieved and he felt the same, although he couldn't imagine why his aunt should want to put herself in harm's way. She could have been safe, staying with her brother's family in Germany in a room of her own, instead of accommodation for refugees. At the time, he couldn't grasp why she should be so attached to her little flat. To that one room she had shared with her husband until his death and where, when their two children were still at home, the four of them had lived together. The few times he and his parents had gone to Karlovac to see her, she had hardly ever stirred from that room of hers – she had just sat on her sofa all day long. Presumably she spent the war years on that sofa.

Looking back, he feels ashamed at how distant he once felt from his aunt and her fate. But Ana was different. He wanted to know about her life. She had nothing to reproach him with on that score. Quite the opposite. She was the one who held back, who even resented hearing him read from the morning paper. Yet he couldn't help feeling that someone forced to leave her childhood home and endure being shot at in her new one might feel persecuted by fate.

"Your wartime experiences," he said, "don't confer moral superiority, you know." The look in her eyes was steely when they met his. Her lips moved, and he realised that she had been about to say something, but changed her mind. She shook her head in disbelief, glanced at the window and got up to leave.

Uncertain what to do next, he stayed in the kitchen after she closed the door behind her. He observed her cup and a spot of dried coffee close to the rim. Later, the brownish stain on the white china would regain its shape in his mind and stand out clearly, so very clearly that the rest of the memory would appear to materialise around it. He would want to get a cloth and wipe the rim clean, but the mark would not be shifted.

He observed the plate covered with breadcrumbs, and next to it a knife with its blade thinly coated with strawberry jam. Her indoor shoes were under the table by her chair, where she had pulled them off. The left shoe looked forlorn, lying on its side near a table leg.

He sat in the middle of her kitchen, trying to find a source of strength. It frightened him that she had left. He feared that the woman who returned would be someone he wouldn't know. He soon lost all sense of how long he had been sitting there. He blamed himself for being so insensitive, and tried to find the right words. He wanted to apologise. He longed for the sound of a key turning in the lock, of her footsteps on the floorboards. He longed for the familiarity of homecoming. He long for those reassuring noises: coat hangers being handled, outdoor shoes being put away and keys being placed on the shelf. His wait lasted for an eternity.

When she came into the kitchen, she stood by the table and he saw in her a weariness he did not recognise. Her skin was drained of colour and her eyes somehow sat deeper in their sockets. Had the light changed? Or his perception of her? She held her cup with both hands, as if it were a heavy weight, glanced into it and emptied it in one gulp.

Yet again, he thinks about Ana's words. He wonders if Ana would have interpreted the behaviour of the judges and counsel for the prosecution differently. The judge on the left, who kept his arms crossed on his chest most of the time, the prosecutor's assistant who shuffled notes across the table with such indifference, the presiding judge who regularly interrupted the defendant in a tone of voice one might call brusque, directing him to make sure that he paused before answering, to avoid making the interpreter's job unnecessarily difficult, ... *as I told you before*. Would she have thought them arrogant? Would she have perceived these people as representing victors' justice and their gestures as humiliating? What about him? As an onlooker, is he part of this other world which conspires against hers? No, she couldn't think that, of course he has never conspired against her, he has loved her, he loves her. He would do anything for her. Ana, you know you're wrong.

"Well, it's tragic," the professor said, "but it's a historical fact that Serbia is, it seems, the only country that hasn't faced up to the need for national catharsis. By now, it has been left alone with its guilt complex, isolated from the rest of the world, for almost twenty years. The end of the war didn't offer a new beginning for the Serbs: the same old war leader still held office and, even after his fall, they had only a brief glimpse of hope before Djindjić was shot. Try to imagine what it all meant for the young in Serbia. They suffer to this day. In their generation, they're the only ones who aren't allowed to travel freely in Europe, because Europe rejects their country."

One week after the last time he saw Ana, he talked once more to the professor. He didn't tell him about what he'd found out about Ana. He didn't admit that he could hardly sleep because of the thoughts forever turning over in his head. He didn't explain that he felt betrayed and constantly had to ask himself what had really happened. He didn't mention that he hadn't eaten for days and spent most of the time in bed, longing for reassurance that it would turn out to be a misunderstanding, that one day the doorbell would ring and she would stand outside. He hoped she'd at least phone or write him a letter.

To this day, he has been waiting for her to tell him about herself and to try, for the sake of their love, to make him understand.

Counsel for the defence seems to speak in a different tone of voice now. He sounds gentler than the previous day, when he was examining Šimić. Mr Nurzet speaks more slowly, more calmly and pauses frequently, as if he wants the woman in the witness stand to take her time, to think before she answers and take care not to say anything rash.

"Mrs Šimić, try to recall April 1992 and tell us where you were at the relevant time."

When he stepped into the public gallery that morning, he had no idea that Ana's mother would enter the courtroom just a little later. He saw an elderly woman come in through the door to the right of the judges' bench. She was visibly ill at ease. For a short while, she stood looking at the judges, until one of them gestured to the table and the court attendant escorted her to it. "Mrs Šimić, please sit down." It was only when the judge spoke her name that he realised who she was. He went rigid for a moment. It hadn't occurred to him that Ana's mother would be summoned to appear in court. But now she's there, sitting some two metres away from him, with just a sheet of glass between them. She wears a white blouse and a black ankle-length skirt. Her hair is grey, unlike Šimić's. He didn't think of her looking like this; he imagined her to be younger and less plump.

It feels unsettling and improbable to see Ana's parents in this place, isolated behind a pane of glass. He can observe them, nothing else. In his mind, Ana joins them: father, mother, daughter – and, for the first time, he's glad that she isn't here. It would be unbearable to watch the whole family, in this place, all three of them united in the courtroom. The daughter would have come because she believes in the goodness of this man who allowed children to die in a fire. He doesn't want to imagine her appearing as a witness for the defence in this courtroom, facing her father and protecting him. How obligingly she would answer the defence lawyer's questions, describe her father as loving and recall her childhood memories. Not here, in front of all these people – the judges, the prosecution, the defence and the public. He would feel so helpless. He could do nothing but sit there and listen. She would be so close and yet behind that glass. And he would be just another onlooker.

Ana's mother starts to speak twice before her voice picks up enough strength to reply to the defence lawyer's question.

"In April 1992, we were in Belgrade. We had to flee from Višegrad. They started setting houses on fire and everyone who had children had left the town."

"Frau Šimić, you've said: 'We had to flee'. What do you mean by 'we'? Which members of your family came with you?"

"I took my daughter, Ana."

"You said earlier that everyone left the town because houses were set on fire. What do you mean by 'everyone'?"

"At that time, women with children left because they were frightened."

"Are you suggesting that to stay in Višegrad at that time was unsafe? Or do you mean something else? Something more specific?"

"If you had children to look after, it wasn't safe to stay in town. They threatened us. Some of these people had occupied the dam. They wanted to dynamite it and flood all the villages on the Drina."

"Who were the people you're referring to?"

"They were local Muslims. They wanted to flood the town and drown us all."

"In the beginning, you said that houses were set on fire. Please tell the court whose houses they were."

"The Savić house was burnt, I think. Branko's place. That's it, his name was Branko Savić."

"The people whose houses burnt, what ethnic group did they belong to?"

"They were Serbs."

"Did Zlatko, your husband, come with you to Belgrade?"

"No, he stayed behind in our house."

"Had he agreed that you and your daughter should leave?"

"Yes. It was his idea. He said we had to go, because he feared that something would happen to us if we didn't."

It's clear to everyone how very uncomfortable Ana's mother feels about being in the courtroom. She doesn't know where to look, meeting the lawyer's eyes only rarely and fleetingly. She speaks so softly that the judge often has to urge her to come closer to the microphone. She seems frightened of this black device and doesn't touch it, so the lawyer has to walk across and point the microphone towards her mouth.

She has probably never spoken in front of such a large audience. The distress, the sleepless nights, and the journey to a strange place, she has dealt with these things for his sake. In order to see him again? For love? He would have liked to know if they touched each other when they met. Here, in the courtroom, she avoids looking at her husband. Šimić, on the other hand, does not take his eyes off his wife for the entire time.

"What can you tell us about Zlatko's family? Does he have brothers or sisters? And if he does, who are they? Where do they live? Are they younger than him, or older?"

"Zlatko is the firstborn. He has two younger sisters, a brother and a half-sister. One of his sisters lives in Belgrade and the other in Banja Luka. The brother lives in Vardište."

"He has one half-sister, you tell us. Was she on his mother's side or his father's?"

"His father's side."

"So, did Zlatko lose his mother, or did she and his father separate?"

"His mother disappeared when he was eight years old. At least, I think he was eight, but I don't know exactly."

"How do you mean, 'disappeared'?"

"One day she was gone."

"And later your husband's father re-married? Is that correct?"

"Yes, that's correct."

He knows hardly anything about Ana's mother because Ana spoke about her only rarely, as if her mother's role in her upbringing had been negligible or non-existent. In a photograph he once saw, Ana's mother could be seen a couple of paces behind her husband, apparently caught in the frame by accident. And he looked unaware of her presence as he stood there in the foreground, a dominant figure with his gaze fixed on the camera lens.

She is much smaller than him and it needs no special insight to realise that she has lived in his shadow. Perhaps she prefers to stay there; perhaps the shadows simply crept up closer and obscured her. He knows that she was the one who cared for the home and the garden. She has previously been abroad just once, when her husband was invited to Yale to lecture on revenge in Shakespearean drama. They have known each other since childhood. She is the daughter of one of his father's cousins and, from early on, it was obvious to everyone that these two were meant for each other. The one memory of her mother that Ana told him was from the time they fled together. They made their escape quietly. Ana described them on the bus to Belgrade, how she sat by a window with her mother next to her. Nobody spoke while the engine struggled to haul the bus through the mountain passes and made the pane of her window vibrate so much that she pressed her face against it to hold it still.

He's frightened that the courtroom door will open and Ana will come through it. A profound unease comes over him. He has to grip the armrests of his chair to prevent people from noticing how badly his hands shake.

He hasn't seen Ana for weeks. At first he wanted to be alone, to think everything over in peace or, at least, that was what he told himself. But that wasn't all. He felt deceived. She led two lives, one with him and one that excluded him. He found this duplicitous. She did not reciprocate his trust in her. It hurt him, he felt hard done by and hoped that she would take the first step, come to see him one day and stand outside his door, or write to him, or at least speak to him on the phone to explain everything. He was prepared to be understanding, whatever she told him. When she didn't come, he took it to mean that she wouldn't reveal her other life to him because she thought him unworthy of being part of it.

He searched his memory for incidents which supported these doubts of his. He remembered the drive back from the Baltic Sea, when she taught him words in Serbo-Croat: sea – *more*, wind – *vetar*, waves – *talasi*, sand – *pesak*, life – *život*. But not the word for "love". And that would have been the first word to occur to him.

Or that summer's day on the lawn in Tiergarten. Ana pulled her T-shirt up just enough to let the sun reach part of her stomach. She held out her hand and he twisted his fingers in between hers. Then she felt about for the bottle of water, found it, gently freed her hand, unscrewed the top and straightened up almost to sitting position in order to drink. She gazed down at him then. The look in her eyes is etched into his mind, so clear and deep, at odds with the absent expression on her face. Her eyes stayed on him, unrelated to the faint smile that began to hover around her lips. For him, that moment is torn out of the flow of time. Next, with her cheeks full of water, she held out the bottle for him, he took it and drank the rest in one gulp. It seemed to him that happiness flowed into his body with the water. He leapt up, stood over her and prodded her navel gently with his big toe. Her body jerked, she sat up, took his hands and burrowed her face into them. The sun had warmed her skin, and his fingertips picked up its sweaty glaze. "Do you have any idea," he had asked, "just how happy you make me? Do you realise the joy you've brought me by suddenly coming into my life?" He's still sure that her eyes filled with tears. And he believed that her tears were testimony of their love for each other. Or were they just the tearfulness of saying goodbye?

He asked if she was all right, not if she loved him. Another person's love for him seemed such an unsettled, fragile thing, like a mobile which the slightest touch can set off in incessant, self-generated motion. He had previously been in love with a woman who blamed him because, she said, he wouldn't leave the tender plant of love time to grow and flourish. He made love wither away. The phrase stayed in his mind; he couldn't rid himself of it. The absurd thing was that his love for Ana felt as solid as a rock, indestructible. That was why he didn't question her directly. He didn't want to throw his weight around. He would say, "You know, don't you, that I've never loved anyone as I love you?" And she would touch his face, running her index finger along the ridge of his nose, across his lips, then stroking his hair away from his forehead.

Perhaps he reproaches her, above all, for treating his memories of her so carelessly. He cannot let go, not even weeks later. His journey to The Hague has been nothing but a desperate attempt to understand. The prospect of seeing her father frightened him. He feared it, because out of his love for Ana he might feel protective towards a man who had led forty-two human beings to their death. He feared it, because he might betray his own moral convictions. And he also feared that he might doubt the veracity of a woman who had survived the fire and returned as a witness, only because he longed so much for Ana's love that he would do anything to recapture it.

For the same reason, he dreaded discovering evil in the man who was Ana's father and come to detest him.

If Ana were to step inside the public gallery, look around and see him there, she would surely realise how seriously he has taken all this. How would she respond to him? And he to her? What would his first words be? Or hers? "I hoped to find you here," she might say. And he might reply, "Ana, you were right all along, all this has nothing to do with us."

The defence lawyer pauses, when his female colleague pushes a note across the table. He quickly reads the message and nods. Then he turns to his witness.

"Mrs Šimić, would you please describe how your husband behaved when under the influence of alcohol?"

"It was bad for him, because after a few days, he'd no longer know what he was saying. He mumbled. It didn't really matter as long as he was with his family. He never harmed us, and he loved his daughter. It was just that drinking did him no good."

"When you say that drinking did him no good, what exactly do you mean?"

"After two or three days he couldn't take food any more. He was no longer aware of what he was saying."

"Can you recall when he started drinking to excess and when the effect on him required treatment for the first time?"

"He started drinking when our son died."

"How old was your son at the time? What were the circumstances of his death?"

"He was sixteen years old and had gone on a skiing holiday in Slovenia. A trip organised for young people. He was out skiing and had a bad fall. When they found him, he was already dead."

Nothing worse can befall parents than the loss of a child. He wonders how Ana's mother came to terms with her son's death. Was she still grieving, deep inside? And how did Ana feel? He knows someone who was sixteen when his brother died. The hurt never went away and, to this day, that man feels guilty because he cannot explain why he's alive and his younger brother dead. What about Ana? Why was it that an acquaintance could speak to him about his brother's death and how it weighed heavily on his mind, while Ana could not bring herself to mention it at all?

He observes Ana's mother, as if the answer might be read in her face. He tries to imagine her as a young woman, at the age Ana is now. But he fails. Life has sapped her strength, he can see that. He would like to know what her true reaction was when she learnt of her husband's arrest. Did she have any suspicion that there might not have been a mistake? Did she secretly believe that he might be guilty? Was it even possible that she had understood him, because she realised the extent to which suffering had driven them both insane?

Soldiers from the NATO Stabilisation Force had rented the house belonging to Ana's grandparents and built by them just before the Bosnian War. It was only about ten metres from the Šimićs' place. Now Ana's mother speaks of how well they got on with the French soldiers. They exchanged greetings, then became friends, she says, actually using the word – friends. When the soldiers had something to celebrate, birthdays or Christmas, she would walk across to their quarters and cook for them. She brought them tomatoes from her own garden. Her lawyer asks if the soldiers had known her husband's name, and she replies, "Of course. They all knew who we were and everyone knew Zlatko."

"Did any official, under whatever authority, tell your husband that he was under suspicion or that he was being investigated?"

"No, never."

"Did your husband ever mention in your presence that he was afraid of being taken away for questioning?"

"No, never."

After the midday break, Mr Bloom, the prosecutor, takes over. He too wants to speak about the French soldiers.

When did they leave the house of her parents-in-law, he asks. She answers that they left just after her husband was arrested.

"From the moment of your husband's arrest, soldiers were no longer stationed in the house next door – is that correct?"

"Yes."

Mr Bloom gives her a sidelong glance and then ostentatiously shakes his head.

"Mrs Šimić, at least at that point in time, it must surely have occurred to you that the soldiers were in your in-laws' house for six months because they were ordered to arrest your husband and also obtain as much information as possible about your nephew Marić, who – as you know – is charged with having set fire to the building in question."

"No, I didn't. I truly had no idea. I only knew that they were staying in our house, but I didn't know why they were there."

"Previously, in connection with questions concerning your nephew, you said, 'I've heard that he's supposed to be involved in arson, but I don't know anything about it. I wasn't there. I haven't seen him.' I'd like to ask you now when you first heard that Milan Marić had been involved in acts of arson?"

"I don't know. Stories began doing the rounds and the newspapers were on to it. My brother-in-law once showed me an article, but by then I was already living in Belgrade."

"During this trial, we have heard other witnesses state that several houses were set on fire. So, referring to what I understand you to have said earlier, you believed that people died during the fire of which you spoke, that is, the house fire in Pionirska Street. Is that right?"

"I don't know who died."

"Do you believe that people died during the fire you've spoken about?"

"I read about it in the paper afterwards. I don't know anything else. I wasn't there."

"I would like to know if you believe that people died there or not."

"I assume they did. I've no idea, not really. I don't know."

She feels under pressure, that much is obvious, the tone of her voice has changed. It sounds dismissive, nervous and despairing at the same time. Perhaps she didn't realise that her statement could be used against her husband. Perhaps now, in the presence of judge and prosecutor, she has become aware that appearing in court won't help him.

He believes her. She doesn't know if people died or not. She must have read about the deaths of the Hasan-ovićs; if a newspaper gives the name of a suspect, it will surely also report any fatalities. But she forgot, because she didn't want to know. She never questioned anything. She wouldn't have wanted to know if her husband was involved in this crime. When he was arrested, she didn't enquire about the charge. Was that for fear that he might be guilty?

During the past weeks, he has reflected again and again on what he would have done in Ana's place. It's so hard to imagine one's own father as a murderer, or an accomplice to murder. A murder that he denies any part in. Shouldn't his son be ready to believe him? Should it be up to the son to investigate his father's guilt or innocence? Who would insist upon a son searching for evidence against his father?

Mr Bloom keeps his eyes fixed on Ana's mother.

"In a year, how frequent would his drinking bouts be?"

"It varied. He could often go for five or six months without alcohol, but at other times he wouldn't last that long."

"When he was drinking to excess, were you able to discuss things with him? Could you speak to him about matters concerning your daughter or your house?"

"Why do you ask? Of course I could. Early on when he drank hard, it wasn't easy, but then he'd stop and everything would be normal again. So, yes, we could talk together."

"Have you ever quarrelled with him when he was drunk?"

"No."

"Did he ever shout at his daughter while drunk?"

"No, he's crazy about his daughter."

"I note that, according to you, the only problematic aspect of your husband's drinking was that he stopped eating and lost weight. Apart from that, there seems to have been no other ill effects for his family. Have I understood you correctly?"

"Yes. Only that it was bad for him. That his health was affected."

"Mrs Šimić, you have mentioned earlier that your husband found the sight of hurt or crippled people extremely troubling. My next question concerns his role as a host. When there was something to celebrate and you planned to serve up chicken, or perhaps lamb or pork, presumably your husband, as the man of the house, would slaughter the animal?"

"You're right that it's our custom to slaughter a lamb or pig on such an occasion, but Zlatko never did it. He just couldn't make himself do it. Every time, we had to ask a neighbour. I remember that when the soldiers who lived in our house had something to celebrate and wanted grilled lamb, we asked our neighbour because Zlatko didn't have the heart to kill a lamb or a chicken. Zlatko has never slaughtered an animal."

"Do you know the reason why?"

"He has an aversion to that kind of thing. He doesn't like it at all. The very thought of killing an animal is a torment for him."

Šimić looks on impassively as he follows his wife's performance. He sits straight-backed and soberly dress-ed, his hair neatly combed. Unresponsive and unemotional, just intensely attentive. In the gallery, many clearly feel ill at ease. Mrs Šimić's last few sentences have triggered a restiveness you can't miss: in the row in front, a man puts his head in his hands, another removes his headphones. In his row, someone's foot is jerking and a woman leans back in her seat and closes her eyes.

The judge tells Mrs Šimić to leave the court. She looks around for someone to help her and is escorted out by one of the attendants. No doubt she meant well, but now seems to feel lost. Just before she leaves, she turns towards the defendant and tries to catch his eye. He stares fixedly into space. The judge asks for the next witness to be called.

On the way back from the Baltic coast, he decided to turn off the motorway. He wanted to show her Müritz, the great lake. For many years, it had been the place he went to when the winter in Berlin, with its constant drizzle and grim, grey buildings, made him so depressed that nothing seemed any good. He tried to remember his usual route, but roadworks forced him to follow a diversion. Then, believing that he recognised the road they were on, he almost missed a turning and had to brake sharply. Too late, he noticed the car behind him and realised that his manoeuvre had almost landed it in trouble. He waved apologetically.

They could already see Lake Müritz in the distance. He had read somewhere that the name was derived from a Slav word, *morcze* or "small sea". Ana took her feet off the dashboard. Later, he would often wonder why he'd taken Ana to Müritz and only wished he hadn't. He had simply wanted to show her a beautiful place and decided on an impulse.

"You'll like this," he said and, at that very moment, there was the loud whine of a car engine closing in. He glanced in the mirror. A blue Golf with darkened windows, the car which his earlier carelessness had forced to make an emergency stop, was now hanging on his tail.

"What's up?" Ana asked.

"Just some nutter," he told her.

She turned round to see.

"What does he want?"

"To scare us a little. Look, he's overtaking us now."

In the side-mirror, he saw the car pull out. As it drew alongside, the passenger window opened and they could see two men with smooth-shaven skulls in the front seat. The Golf accelerated, got back in lane and stopped in front of them. He thought for a moment of moving out to overtake, but there was an oncoming car in the other lane. He had to stop.

"What do they want?" Ana asked and locked the doors from the inside.

Four men climbed out of the blue car, one by one. All four wore bomber jackets and rolled-up jeans over high boots. Two of them stayed by their car, one on each side, and one of them went to stand at Ana's door.

He saw Ana's hand grip the door handle. The man on his side of the car knocked on the window. He briefly considered putting his foot down on the accelerator, but that would have meant running over two of them.

"Step outside," said the skinhead who had knocked on the window.

He held onto the steering wheel and stared straight ahead, trying to breathe calmly. One of the two men in front of the car used his foot to pump the bumper up and down. He drew a deep breath and reached out to open the window, but Ana cried, "No! Don't!"

"So, what do I do?" he asked.

"Whatever you do, don't open up."

The guard on the driver's side banged on the roof with the palm of his hand, once, twice and a third time, before bending to look inside their car. He stared at Ana, then at him. "Come on," he said. "I must do something. We can't just sit and wait."

"Drive. Drive off, they'll jump away fast enough," Ana whispered. He felt alarmed – naturally, who wouldn't be in a situation like this? There were four of them and each one was physically stronger than he was. He wound the window down. As he did, he saw Ana close her eyes and clutch at the edge of her seat with her free hand.

The skinhead stared quizzically at him. Then he said, "Look, man, you screwed up. You admit that?" He reached into the car, opened the door and said: "Get out."

Ana's eyes were still closed.

What would happen if he didn't get out, if he simply sat there?

"Come on, out." The man's voice sounded more aggressive now.

He got out.

"Good. Now, you apologise for what you did."

He glanced into the car and realised that Ana was watching him from the passenger seat. He held onto the open door. "I'm really so..." His voice cracked and he had to clear his throat. "I am really sorry."

"Sorry for what?" the skinhead asked, glancing at his mates.

He felt himself blush and glanced quickly up the road in the hope of seeing another car. "I'm really sorry," he then said, "that I braked the car right in front of you."

The big man in bomber jacket and boots scrutinised him. He can still remember that man's gaze, his dark eyes. And he still remembers what he thought at the time: these eyes, with their hint of melancholy, don't fit the scenario. The perception would stay with him, even though, a moment later, he saw only the cold stare of superiority.

"Where are you from?"

"Berlin."

"What I mean is, are you German?"

"Why do you ask?"

"You look a bit like an Eyetie or a Yugo."

He glanced at Ana. And said, "Yes, I am German."

The man seemed to think this over. Then he looked at his mates and nodded in their direction. They all climbed into the Golf and drove off.

After a while, when the Golf was well out of sight, he got back inside. "I'm so sorry," he said, without meeting Ana's eyes.

And she said, "You shouldn't have opened the window."

The next witness, called once Ana's mother left the courtroom, turns out to be male. Ana hasn't come through that door. That's enough for him. He has no idea who this man is, and isn't interested. He takes off his headphones and leaves.

He walks to the beach and finds a place to sit in one of the many cafés, picking a seat from where he can look out over the sea. He orders a pot of tea and stays until darkness falls. Before he goes, he asks the waitress the way to the prison. She shrugs. But surely everyone in the world has heard of the Scheveningen prison for war criminals? "It must be somewhere nearby," he says. "I guess so," she replies, "but I've no idea." She looks to be in her early twenties. "Have you never heard of the war crimes tribunal?" She picks up his cup and puts it on her tray. "Yes, I've heard of it." She looks at him briefly. "Was there anything else?" He shakes his head.

It's colder now, even though the wind has died down. He finds a hotel reception and asks for directions. The man behind the counter quickly checks him over. "You want the United Nations Detention Unit, right?" He nods. The man mentions a couple of street names, and then repeats them in the same order: Gevers Deynootweg, Zwolsestraat. There's a bus, he adds, but it's walking distance. Take the first on the left and go on until you come to the park, then walk through the park. Perhaps, he thinks, it would be better to wait until daylight, but he sets out anyway, in what he hopes is the right direction.

He has to ask twice on the way, but reaches the prison. Tall brick walls. It looks like a fortress. Walls protecting the inmates from the outside world.

He read in a book about the court that the prisoners, who are all charged with war crimes, have created their own private reality behind the walls. It is a world free from ethnic conflicts, where Serbs, Croats and Muslims cook and play games together, and sign birthday cards to each other's relations. The members of this community have fought wars against each other, massacred people of one ethnicity or other, causing distrust among the survivors. Now they get on perfectly well together, as if they want to mock their victims' suffering.

Šimić's cell is somewhere inside this building. Fifteen square metres equipped with shower, WC, washbasin and table. He is allowed to use a computer, but not to connect it to the Internet. He can watch television in his native language, has access to a lending library and also courses in arts, languages or sciences. Perhaps Šimić sits there now with the others, having an evening meal in the kitchen. Or he might be reading quietly.

It occurs to him for the first time that Ana probably visited her father during the week she was away. That was the week just before they went to the seaside together. She never told him that she planned to travel anywhere. It was only when he asked her if she'd like to come along and see a friend on his birthday that she said she wouldn't be around. He asked where she was going. Belgrade, she said, just for a few days. It disappointed him that she hadn't let him know that she was going away, and so soon too. He pointed out that he could have come with her, if only she had told him earlier.

He imagines himself walking up to the prison gate to say that he would like to meet one of the inmates, because he has fallen in love with the man's daughter. Perhaps he could write Šimić a letter and hand it in at the gate. But what would he write?

Herr Šimić, you don't know me. I'm not even sure that you're aware of my existence. Ana may have told you about me, as I got to know her in Berlin. Last February, I fell in love with her. I didn't know then whose daughter she was.

She has told me a great deal about you. You read Shakespeare aloud to her and, in the summer, you used to take her for walks along the banks of the Drina. You taught her angling and how to kill a fish. You played Coltrane and Armstrong records for her, which inspired her to learn the trumpet. And you bought her one, which she played at home in the cellar.

You're always a good man in the stories Ana tells about you. I admit there were times I wished you were my father. I fantasised about the day I would meet you for the first time. Do you know that Ana keeps a photograph of you on the wall next to her desk? It's easy to see that Ana is your daughter. You have the same eyes.

I don't know if you caught sight of me in the courtroom, but then, even if you had, how could you have known who I was? I doubt that Ana has shown you my photo. But I have been watching you during your trial.

When I listened to what you were charged with, I wished you weren't who you are – I wished that the man in the dark suit, who toyed with his tie while a woman spoke of her family burning, was not Ana's father. But I did observe your eyes.

Frankly, I don't know why I'm writing to you. Is it because I hope that the whole thing is a misunderstanding and that you were not on the bridge at that particular time? Do I really want to know you? The prospect of meeting you frightens me.

I haven't seen Ana for weeks now and it's all because of you. You have come between us. But I still think of Ana all the time. Why do I write to you? Perhaps because I would like to know if Ana was mistaken about you.

He is cold and decides to take the bus back. What did he hope to gain by seeing the prison? He has no idea. But then the gate opens and a solitary figure, a woman, steps outside. In the poor light, he sees that she's wearing a coat. A short woman, walking with her eyes fixed on the ground. She is coming towards him. As she crosses the street only a few metres away, he recognises her. Actually, he recognised her at once.

They are the only ones at the bus stop and their eyes meet briefly. She sits down, folding her hands in her lap. He can hardly take his eyes off her. The street light makes her look pale. Close-up, she looks younger than she seemed in the courtroom. He sees her hands, Ana's hands, with their soft fingers, pale and fragile. The rest of her body is different from Ana's. She is shorter, heavier, much plumper. Her stillness is different; there's more tenseness in it.

Then there's the sound of the bus and its headlights sweep across the stop. She goes to sit on an aisle seat near the back. He walks past her, but she takes no notice. He finds a seat two rows behind her.

She must hate it, he thinks, this city and all it stands for. Hate this bus, the houses we're passing, the people who live here in a city that has taken away her husband and perhaps will never let him go. He doesn't know what kind of sentences are meted out to men like Šimić, maybe he'll get ten years or fifteen, or maybe he'll spend the rest of his life locked up. He watches her. When the bus goes rounds a corner, she holds onto the edge of her seat and he sees her hand. There is a wedding ring on it.

"Mrs Šimić, would you please tell us when you married?"

"I've been married for thirty-five years. Thirty-five this year. The wedding was on the 12th of February 1970."

"Tell us when your children were born."

"Our son Milan was born on the 23rd of November 1972 and our daughter Ana on the 15th of June 1980."

"Would you describe your marriage as happy?"

"Yes."

"To this day?"

"Yes."

The bus route crosses half the city. He isn't sure what this journey is all about.

"My mother? Mum took care of the house. Cooked, did the laundry, cleaned. She ran a small shop once, but she gave it up after a while. Do I take after my mother in any way? Everyone has something of their mother in them. But what exactly do you want me to say? Why do you want to know? Why are you so interested?"

"You haven't put her photo on the wall."

"What's that supposed to mean?"

"It just occurred to me."

He recalls that Ana told him she and her mother didn't speak much on that bus journey. Everyone on that bus was very quiet. The passengers were all women and children. Ana's mother kept a plain white plastic bag on her lap, a bag from the baker's shop. Once, she must have brought the bread home in it. Ana only learned later that there was soil in the bag, earth dug up in her mother's garden.

There are so many questions to ask this woman. What is Ana doing? How is she? Where is she? Perhaps they could sit down and talk together in a café. Meanwhile, he stares out through the window at houses and parked cars.

She is almost outside when he leaps up, hurries to the door and manages to jump out just before it closes. What next?

Apart from the two of them, there is no one around. "Mrs Šimić." He needs two attempts before his voice carries. She stops and turns round. Looks at him. He comes closer until he is one or two paces away from her.

"Mrs Šimić," he says.

She only stares at him questioningly. He says, "I'm a friend of Ana's."

She still only looks at him, but nods when he says "Ana".

"I got to know her in Berlin."

She shrugs and now he realises that she doesn't understand English. "Ana," he says.

She nods again.

"Ana, fine?" he asks. "*Dobro?*"

She nods. Then she looks over her shoulder. She says something he doesn't understand. Signs that she must get on. She turns, walks away, hesitatingly at first, then with a more determined step. He stands there for a while, looking after her.

"It wasn't my mother's fault that I was taken away. She didn't want to be on that bus either."

For her birthday, he baked honey cake. It was a Serb recipe he'd found in a cookbook. The cake, decorated with flowers of white icing, was beautifully presented in the photograph. Because it was his first ever cake, he underestimated the cost.

The first instruction was to stir the egg mixture in a *bain-marie*. He didn't know what that meant. Once he had found out, he had to learn that the mixture sets when the water gets too hot. He rolled out the dough, trying to make six equally sized layers of the same thickness. Then, he had to distribute creamy filling over five of the layers and place the sixth on top. At the same time, he was meant to whip the egg whites to stiff peaks and add the syrup. "The whipped egg whites will puff up when they come into contact with the hot syrup," the recipe said, but when he tried it, nothing of the kind occurred. The whites didn't stiffen either. Desperate to make the icing set, he stuck the cake in the freezer compartment. He called his father and asked him to phone his sister in Karlovac for advice. It annoyed him that he couldn't speak her language.

Hours later, the cake was ready, though it looked nothing like the picture. He hoped that Ana would recognise it as Honey Cake anyway, or at least understand how much hard work had gone into its creation.

They went dancing that evening. Or rather, she danced. Most of the time, he leant against the bar next to the dance floor and watched her merging into the dancing crowd, high on alcohol and music. He wished he could switch off that easily. At midnight, they met at the bar to drink her birthday toast. It was the night between the 14th of June. Only much later would he come to realise what a fateful date that was. On that night, sixteen years earlier, the Hasanović family had burnt to death. He wondered about this. Could it be anything more than an unfortunate coincidence? What connection could there possibly be between Ana's birthday and that odious crime? None. But then, later on, he would feel that their champagne celebration was in some way improper.

She was still asleep when he quietly slipped out of bed to go into the kitchen and take the Honey Cake out of the fridge. It was decorated with his version of twenty-eight flowers made of icing. He spread out a white sheet close to the bed and placed the cake on it, together with a knife to cut it with and his gift, a box which looked the right size for a piece of jewellery.

She slept with her face resting on her hand. Even now, asleep, she seemed to hide her toes, one set squeezed in behind the other. He began to count the freckles on her face, trying to find the little one on her lower lip.

The first time he had woken up beside her, he wanted one of her freckles to be his and chose one on her lip. He asked her the word for "freckle". It was something to do with summer and he still remembers the word – *leto* – but what was the other part? "*Pega,*" she said, "*pega.*" He stored the word away, as he did all the words she taught him. The word for "love" he learned later on – *ljubav*. He asked her and she said: "Is that right? You don't know how to say 'love'?" She shook her head in disbelief.

She blinked. Then she turned to lie on her back, opened her eyes and, once she had slowly become fully conscious, he said in English, "Happy Birthday."

She sat up. "Look, a cake."

"Can you see what it is?"

She examined the cake.

"A real Serb Honey Cake," he told her.

"Somehow, I remembered it differently," she said and blew him a kiss.

"Would you like some?"

She nodded and he cut her a slice.

"And what's that?" she asked, pointing to the gift.

"That? It looks like a gift to me."

He picked up the small box, handed it to her and sat down next to her on the bed.

She straightened up, looked at the package from all sides, shook it and said: "I can't work out what it is."

"You've got to work harder then," he said.

She unwrapped it, put the tiny box on the palm of her hand and opened the lid. "What's this?" she asked, holding a round pebble between her fingers.

"Smell it," he told her. "The smell might remind you of somewhere."

She lifted the small stone to her nose, sniffed it and shook her head.

"This isn't any old pebble," he said. "Getting it cost me a lot of effort and lots of phone calls. I had to persuade them to find me this stone – and most of the time we didn't understand each other. This is a pebble..." he paused and looked into her eyes. "This is a pebble from Lumbarda Bay."

She still seemed baffled.

"Ana," he said. "I'd like to come with you to Lumbarda and the journey would be my gift to you."

She stared at the pebble, then closed her hand around it.

He watched her face in profile. The ridge of her nose, so very straight, the high cheekbones, her lips pressed together.

She breathed in three times before she turned to him and asked, "When?"

He watches as, behind the glass, the court rises and the judges leave the room in an orderly file. By now, almost everyone else has left the public gallery and the guard glances at him reproachfully. He apologises and hands in his headphones.

He's not sure what to do next and ponders whether to leave for the day or come back and follow the trial after the lunch break. Standing in the foyer, still deep in thought, he suddenly realises that someone is talking to him. It's a young woman with short, dark hair, probably about his own age.

She tells him in English that she's sure she saw him here yesterday, and asks if he's following the entire Šimić trial. He nods, asking himself if he has noticed her before. But he can't remember, so she probably sat in one of the rows behind him.

"I'm Aisha," she says and they shake hands. She offers him a cigarette, but he declines. She asks where he's from. Berlin, he says.

"Oh, good. Let's speak German instead. Shall we go outside? I could do with some fresh air."

He holds the door open. She walks down the few steps and then stops. Some of the other visitors leave, presumably off to lunch in the city.

"Why are you here?" she asks.

"I wanted to know what this sort of trial is like."

"Are you a law student?"

"No, I'm not."

"I'm pretty sure most of the people in there study law."

"Have you been here from the start?"

"Yes." She looks at him. "And you?"

"I was here during the first week. I came back the day before yesterday."

"Why did you choose this particular trial?"

He watches her as she lights a cigarette, pulling up the collar of her blouse to shelter the flame from the wind.

"Just chance. It could've been another one."

She clutches her shoulders and is clearly feeling the cold, so he asks if she would like to go back inside. She looks around, and then asks, "Why don't we go somewhere to eat?"

They collect their jackets from the lockers. She pulls a woollen hat down over her ears and pushes her hands into her pockets.

After wandering the streets for a while, they find a small Chinese restaurant. The waitress escorts them to the only free table, next to an aquarium full of energetic, brightly phosphorescent fish. At the next table, a man in a suit reads a newspaper written in Chinese script, while bending over a small bowl. Aisha pulls a packet of cigarettes and a lighter from her pocket and puts them on the table.

"Berlin is great," she says. "I went to live there once, years ago. An aunt of mine lives there, in Kreuzberg."

"How long were you living in Germany?"

"Seven years, from '92 to '99."

"And then?"

"We all went back to Bosnia. My sister and I would have liked to stay on, but my parents weren't happy. We were living in a hostel for refugees, the four of us in one room. My father couldn't find a job and my mother was cleaning people's houses. We had our own house in Bosnia. My father was a teacher there, and my mother ran a small shop. They would never have got used to living in Germany."

"Where do you live now?"

"In Sarajevo, or rather, my parents are there. I've lived in London for the last year."

Aisha picks up the teaspoon to push the tea bag down into the hot water. When she lets go, it floats back to the surface.

"Have you ever been to Bosnia?" she asks.

"No, I haven't."

"Bosnia is a lovely country, you know. There are mountains and high plateaus, lots of rivers and deep gorges. Not many people know that."

A small elongated fish, with grey, black-spotted skin, emerges from under a stone, first snaking across the fine gravel and then climbing. The waitress sets their table with plates and a hotplate. She serves two spoonfuls of rice onto each plate. He nods his thanks.

The snake-like fish has disappeared. He can't see it anywhere. Perhaps it has crawled back inside its little cave under the stone.

"I still haven't quite understood why you're here," she says.

He raises his glass, drinks a mouthful.

"My father's family comes from Karlovac," he then says. "They were there when the war broke out. But at the time, I didn't think the war particularly interesting."

"Do you have a guilty conscience?"

"No. Well, maybe. Yes. I don't know."

He observes her as she lifts her fork, hesitates for a moment, opens her mouth and slowly begins to chew.

"Has it occurred to you that Šimić could be innocent?" he asks.

She puts the fork down on her plate, straightens her body and looks at him. "Is that a serious question?"

"In court, everyone is innocent until proven guilty. It could be that he …"

"Šimić is a bastard, a criminal who deliberately led these people to their death. He's guilty, just like so many others who haven't been brought to trial and still live in the houses they occupied after they chased the true owners away, or killed them. Even if it can't be proven in court that Šimić did it, which would be crazy, he'd still be guilty. He knows that and everybody else in the court-room knows it too. So, to you it's perhaps just another procedure, a legal process with special rules. Rules which say that he's not a criminal, but an alleged criminal. What's 'alleged' supposed to mean, anyway? Possible? A possible criminal? And are all the others, too, the even guiltier ones – if it's possible to grade guilt like that – the guiltiest, those who are worse than everyone else? Do you have any idea how it offends me that the dead are being counted and the numbers compared, as if it were a competition? Like, this one has killed three people, but that one has killed a hundred, and the very worst of them all has killed a hundred thousand. What you people are doing is offering these men a measure to use in their world, something to brag to each other about – to climb up that perverse hierarchy of theirs. Comparisons are made all the way up to the top people, so Karadžić was the worst, or perhaps Milošević, and then comes Mladić, and then one way or another you establish that Šimić only ranks one hundred and forty on the scale of evil. Why, he hasn't killed anyone with his own hands. And of course the whole lot of them are only alleged criminals until the three judges decide that they're guilty. Can't you see how absurd all this is? What do these judges know? Where were they when hundreds of thousands of people were being pushed out of their homes and chased away, when people were murdered, children and pregnant women among them, and when the others, whose bodies were still alive, realised that their whole existence was ruined, their homeland lost and with it their families, their friends, their faith and any chance of a happy life? At that time, these lawyers and judges were sitting in front of their TV screens, maybe taking an interest, maybe not. Anyway, now they sit on the courtroom bench and decide whether the people who are responsible for everything that happened are guilty and should be punished or not, as the case might be. Proven beyond reasonable doubt, isn't that the phrase? And so perhaps in the end it will be enough to show an entry in a hospital record which states that a certain Zlatko Šimić was admitted to such-and-such hospital at the time of the crime. Because it's written down on a piece of paper, it becomes a fact, as opposed to hearsay. People are subjective and likely to be guided by their emotions, and their statements and recollections aren't verifiable, because they haven't taken note of the exact date and time of day, or get muddled about which day was which. Can you order your memories by the day they happened? There are quite a few people around who don't even know which day their parents died. You know, there's one thing I'll never understand. Why must they always doubt what the witnesses have to say? Why do they have to make people fumble for words in front of everyone else? 'Are you certain that three men were present? Or were there perhaps only two? And, besides, you have stated he wore a black hat, but now you say his hat was dark brown.' Why should it matter what colour the hat was? These people have experienced it all, watched with their own eyes when women and children were murdered, heard them scream and felt the fear of death, but still they're expected to be quite certain whether the hat was black or dark brown. And details like that might well decide the outcome of the trial and determine if Šimić is guilty or not guilty. To my mind, it's cynical."

He prods his portion of rice with his fork, finding it hard to meet her eyes. He senses that the tension in her body is giving way; she's no longer sitting upright and her shoulders are drooping. He looks at her as she stares absently into the aquarium.

He looks at it, too. The snake-like fish has come out of its cavity, just a bit, before calmly stretching out on the gravel. He can't bear this lassitude, he wants the fish to get moving, but doesn't know why he finds it so hard to sit watching while the strange fish just lies there, pretending to be dead. He observes it and tries to get eye contact with it, although he has no idea if it's possible to do that with a fish. He has no idea of how the world is perceived through fish optics, especially the world beyond the aquarium. Perhaps everything outside it seems blurred. Perhaps he should knock on the glass. Fish are meant to be sensitive to vibrations in the water.

But it doesn't even twitch when he knocks. He taps the glass a few more times with the knuckle of his index finger, but there's still no reaction from the fish. Then he notices the look of irritation on Aisha's face, and finds the situation uncomfortable. What is she thinking? That he isn't interested in what she has just said?

She glances at her watch. "They've already started. We should get going." She waves to the waitress.

The public gallery is half full. Aisha goes to a seat in a row at the rear. She puts the headphones on at once, while he takes in the stillness of the room, a cough here and there, a throat cleared and, filling the air, the monotonous drone of the headphones. He looks at Aisha, who is next to him. She sits strangely upright, even a little stiffly, her hands resting on her thighs and her eyes fixed on the glass screen as if entranced. She might even stop breathing, he thinks, so rigid does she look.

She is very different from Ana. Not so tall, her round face fuller and her body less finely boned, the only real similarity is her dark hair and the way she has pushed some strands into place behind her ears. Although she sits so still, she is noticeably restless; a slight, rapid quivering starts from somewhere inside her and moves through her body in waves, as if opening her mouth would be all she needed to let the tension out. He fears that any moment now she will turn to him and ask why he's staring at her. What's wrong? But he feels sure he isn't the reason why she is upset, but rather that this place makes her tremble. Perhaps she has some personal stake in the trial.

It strikes him that he has never before wondered about the source of Ana's inner calm, a calm that has fascinated him from the first time they met. He remembers Ana reading in the theatre cloakroom, the picture of stillness. But that sense of her being at peace with herself baffles him. It doesn't fit. Perhaps it wasn't inner peace, but tiredness. Had she just been very tired that evening, when they met for the first time?

And he recalls wanting to know about the bombing of Belgrade and asking her if she hadn't thought of leaving the city at the time. She replied, "Everyone here asks me that. Sure, I could've left Belgrade, but I simply didn't fancy going. Perhaps it sounds odd, but that's how it was. To live in Belgrade at the time wasn't safe, but I was so tired. Perhaps that's the reason. I was simply tired and kept thinking that this can't go on much longer, or else there'll be no one left."

Aisha watches him, at least she has turned her head towards him and seems to be looking at him, but he isn't sure if she really is. She says nothing. And he doesn't know what to say. Their eyes lock briefly, then she looks away and stares again at the courtroom behind the glass.

For the first time, he imagines that Ana is sitting next to him, here in this place. Suddenly he can see it all. He would have walked up the stairs just a step or two behind her, he would have handed her a set of headphones before pointing to a row with free places and ushered her gently towards one of the seats with his hand on her shoulder. He would have helped her with the headphones and sat down next to her. They would have shared the entire experience. Would she support her father with daughterly tenderness or would she be furious with him? Despite being desperately anxious to work it out, he doesn't feel sure. Would he have touched her? Perhaps he might have put his hand on hers, just very lightly, without squeezing it, so that she could sense his warmth, his presence. He would show her that he's standing by her, supporting her. Not to encourage her on all points, in no way could he claim that it was unjust for her father to be behind that glass screen, or that her father was a truly loveable man, or that he, for one, didn't trust the witnesses. He could not say or do anything to suggest that he believes her father to be innocent.

Did she believe in her father's innocence? What would have been her reason for coming with him to The Hague? Would it be to learn the truth? Would she trust the witness statements about her father? How much did she actually know of what took place place in Višegrad at the time?

In his vision of Ana and himself, he sees the pair of them sitting side by side in silence. And afterwards, out in the street together, they would talk about other things. Perhaps he would ask her if she'd like a walk by the sea or if she's hungry – something like that.

How would you feel seeing your own father in there, behind a pane of glass, and knowing full well that everybody took him for a criminal and wondered what kind of human being could do the things he did? Maybe some people are speculating about the criminal's family and how they've reacted to his crime. He has turned them into victims. This is the real change to his family. Victimised, they will spend the rest of their lives in the perpetrator's shadow. Can anyone forgive that?

It would be so much easier for him, had she ever expressed some doubts about her father, had she never created that image of her loving Dad. If only she had told him that he was given to outbursts of rage, as one of his neighbours has put on record. And that he could be unfair, and her mother, too often, was the target. The neighbour described a party where she contradicted him on some point and he shouted at her in front of everyone. It was known that he expected to be waited on, to be served his food. And if he wanted the salt, she would fetch it from the house. Why didn't Ana tell him about any of this? Her silence has put him in the position of prosecutor, who in the end will shatter the untarnished world she has defended for so long. He would tell her that her father is not a good man, whatever she believes. He would have to point out that a man who leads women and children to their death cannot be full of love. She picked him for this role – picked someone who, at the time, had been so far away – of all people, someone who had led another life in another world. It was downright wicked of her to demand that he should deliberate on moral questions, talk about conscience and claim for himself, as she must see it, the right to make judgements without knowing what had happened, without having been there at the time, without knowing her father and without really knowing her. She would feel attacked by him. His only other option is silence. But how can he stay silent in the face of all that has happened? If she regarded him as uninvolved, this might explain her behaviour when she finally told him, standing by the bookshelf while he sat on the bed. It could be why she didn't come to him, didn't sit down next to him and put her arms round him, didn't kiss him or even hold his hand, didn't want to talk about it and didn't cry as you'd expect of someone who had carried this burden for nine months. You would think it would all have suddenly come pouring out, that she would have wept uncontrollably when the sadness she'd bottled up inside her finally spilled out into the open. You would have expected her to scream, hammer her fists on the wall, tear the books from the shelf and then run from the room, leaving him to hear the front door slam a little later. That would have been easier for him: he could have taken her in his arms, hugged her tight and held her wrists down to stop her from hitting out. He could have pressed her face to his chest and freed her cheeks from strands of damp hair. He could have run after her, caught up with her in the street, grabbed her wrist as she ran and pulled her close, and, though she might well have fought him at first, she would have then clung to him and he would have wrapped her in his coat. They would have stood there while people walked past them, holding each other until he finally said, "Come, let's go now."

Ana looked at him. Searching his memory, he tries to visualise her hands as they were at the time she stood in front of the bookshelf, but it's impossible, because he simply cannot escape the sensation of meeting her gaze, her cool, clear gaze, so hostile it paralysed him. He retains the image of her eyes, nothing else, as if they were detached from the rest of her body. He dwells on this from time to time. Was she not at least holding onto the bookshelf? He's not sure, but thinks not and has instead come to believe that she stood there, in her separate space, upright and grounded in herself.

When Ana left the room, he got up hesitatingly. He saw the old edition of *King Lear* on the bookshelf, the book she had given him on one of their first evenings together and in which he had seen her father's writing for the first time. He stood by the bookshelf. One step closer to the desk and he would be face to face with her father's photograph.

He went over to the window and looked out. The woman on the third floor of the building opposite was standing in the kitchen with her back to him, opening cupboard doors, presumably looking for something. Then she turned round, stood still for a moment as if lost in her own kitchen, before walking away and disappearing from sight. He heard someone's footsteps in the courtyard and the clatter of a dustbin lid.

The flat was quiet. He didn't know where Ana was. He hadn't heard the front door go, so she could only be in the bathroom or the kitchen. What could she be doing? More footsteps in the yard, the person who had taken rubbish down must be walking back. No more sounds. Nothing moved. The kitchen across the way was still empty. A cupboard door hung open; the woman must have forgotten to close it.

He turned to the wall next to the desk and glanced at Šimić. Seeing that face was hard, because he felt betrayed. It had all been in vain, his vision of how they would sit together in harmony at the garden table, his hope of discovering in this man something of what he, as a son, had always missed. And he had been so grateful for Ana.

He has wished so often for something to remember her by, something of hers that he could touch. Apart from a small stone, he has nothing. No book, no clothes left in his flat, no object that she had given him. She had never given him a gift, though she had told him to keep the stone after he had spotted it on her bookshelf and asked what it meant. Surely gifts are part of loving someone? He had been bringing her things all the time: white or red roses, books he had wanted her to read. He had even written her a poem. He had always hoped she would surprise him with a small present, just once. A token of love. But, in the end, he had nothing to remember her by, except his own memories of her and the taste of Sarma.

He walked past the kitchen, where nothing had been tidied away; two plates were still on the table, and the mugs and scattered crumbs. The two chairs had been pulled back a little. There was coffee in the pot, cold by now. He put on his shoes and coat, and wound a scarf around his neck. The bathroom door was shut. He held his breath, trying to listen. Not a sound. He closed his eyes for a moment, then opened the door and left her flat.

For days, he waited for her to phone. It was all he did – wait, mostly lying on the bed. He didn't eat, but when he couldn't bear staying in bed, he walked the streets. He would pass the tree in the park where they had lain together on the grass, sit down on a seat outside the café where he'd bought her coffee. He usually stayed there for a long while before going back home. He checked the downstairs letterbox every time he left his flat or returned to it, and when he walked up the last flight of stairs to his landing, he would close his eyes briefly, hoping that when he opened them he would see a note stuck to his door.

He can remember how fast his heart was beating the day he saw from below the outline of a figure sitting on the landing outside his flat. When he got up the stairs, it turned out to be a neighbour who had forgotten his key.

He phoned her shortly before his first visit to The Hague. She didn't answer. He phoned her when he got back from The Hague and, just as he was near giving up, she answered. "Ana," he said. She was silent. "I …" he mumbled and didn't know what to say next, even though he had thought endlessly about this call. Then he said, "It's time we talked." She replied, "Yes, it's time we did." He said, "It makes me happy to hear your voice again." And she responded, "I'm glad that you called." He said,

"Ana, perhaps we can forget what happened." "That's the problem. I can't forget." "Ana, all this has nothing to do with us." "But it has to do with me and that's why it affects us."

To him, the silence on the line seemed to last for an eternity. And he feared his voice would take on the earnest tone he wanted to avoid. He had tried to sound relaxed to make their talk easier, but her silence unsettled him.

Like him, she'd had a couple of weeks to think about things, time enough for her to put them into focus. He felt that by now she must surely have found a way to speak about what had happened. And that it would have become as clear to her as it was to him that the day she told him should not become their last one together.

"I…" he said, "I'd like to know how you are."

He wondered if her language also had a word for stillness between two people. He could hear her breathing and could almost feel a gentle puff of air tickling his ear. He imagined Ana holding the receiver. Recalled her narrow nose, pale skin and serious eyes. It surprised him how quickly he was coming to enjoy being close to her again. He wished that he could stay on the line to her for hours on end.

He sensed she was about to say something, a tone of voice only, half a syllable. Later he would try to work out the word she had intended to use. He played around with a thousand possibilities, but to be honest, he couldn't even be certain that the sound she'd made was consciously articulated, that it was actually meant to begin a word. Then he heard the click as she put her receiver down. True, she had hesitated a little and he held on until the disconnection signal penetrated his awareness and he too ended the call.

He phoned his father. It cost him to overcome his resistance and he couldn't see why his father, of all people, should be able to help him. The old man had never taken his relationships seriously, neither with girls nor, later, with women. Earlier, he had always refused to say who he was going out with, or even to talk more generally about love. Now and then, his father would ask him about his love life and, every time, he replied, "Just fine."

He had mentioned Ana to his parents, but not told them that her father was a war criminal. That was something he wouldn't even tell his best friend. He wanted to keep the secret between Ana and himself, because he thought this would help them to think clearly about it and what it meant to them.

As always his father's voice answered with his surname, and as always he sounded as if he had been disturbed.

"So it's you," his father said.

"It's me."

"Good. I was in the sitting room anyway."

"I'd like to ask you something."

"Are you in trouble?"

This was clearly his big worry. The kind of trouble his father had in mind included financial problems, a car accident or a broken fridge. Things he could deal with.

What was he supposed to say? That he was in love with the daughter of a Serb war criminal? He doubted his father would even begin to grasp the implications.

"I'd like to know why you never thought it worthwhile for me to learn Croat. And why haven't you tried to make me feel more at home in your old country? Why be so detached from the place you came from? It's something I'd like an answer to."

The line went silent. Then his father said: "You were born *here*, you've grown up *here*. This country is *your* home."

"But you were born in Croatia. That's where you grew up. Doesn't that mean anything to you?"

"Why would you think it doesn't mean anything to me?"

"Because you've never shown any interest. Other people visit the Croatian Cultural Society or read Croatian newspapers. You didn't even pay much attention to the war."

"Look here, my lad," his father said. "I came to this country because I wanted to make something of my life. When you take a step like that, you have to make up your mind. It won't do to try to belong here, there and everywhere, or you'll end up not living anywhere properly. And as for the war, you should thank your lucky stars you saw nothing of it. We were all lucky. You've got no reason to complain. You've done well enough here."

It annoyed him that his father didn't understand what he really meant. It wasn't about him or his son, but that's how the old man always managed to make it sound.

"How's your girlfriend?" his father asked.

"Fine."

"Good! I'm glad that you're happy. Did she like your cake?"

He needed to think for a moment before he realised what cake his father was talking about. He hadn't thought about it since he'd called his father to ask for his aunt's advice on how to bake that special cake.

"Yes, she did," he said.

"My sister wanted to know who you were baking for."

"What did you tell her?"

"For a woman."

"And what did she say to that?"

"She was pleased that you'd found yourself a lady friend."

"And did you mention that she's a Serb?"

"I told her your girlfriend is German."

It seemed a bizarre flight of fancy to turn Ana into a German woman, an Anna like so many others. If his father met Ana, he would understand the absurdity of it.

"She's no German," he said. "Why did you say that?"

"Because your aunt couldn't have coped with anything different. You know, don't you, that the Serbs were shooting at her house? Or didn't you hear about that?"

He hadn't, but it seemed of no consequence.

He has no sense of how long he has been staring straight ahead. Mr Bloom, the prosecutor, is standing at his desk. Cross-examination of the witnesses is in full flow.

A clean-shaven, grey-suited man is at the witness seat. He appears to be in his late forties and is wearing glasses. His hand movements are restrained. Šimić is there too, just as he has been every day so far. But he seems older today, as if he has aged suddenly, from one day to the next. He looks tired, his face is pale and drawn. The light falling on him has a strangeness about it. On previous occasions, he has appeared distant, but deliberately so, as if to punish others with his disdain. Now the impression he gives is of a man who has simply withdrawn into himself, deep in thought.

He nudges Aisha to alert her, then gestures for her to take the headphones off.

"What's this about?" he whispers.

"He's a psychologist, I think. He treated Šimić when he was taken to the clinic with his broken leg."

He nods a thank you and they both put their headphones back on.

"At the time, I diagnosed the patient's condition as psychosis type 298.9, which was in accordance with the *International Classification of Diseases* after the *Ninth Revision, Clinical Modifications*. The numbers have in fact been changed since then. At the time, the 298.9 group included forms of so-called Unspecified or Atypical Psychoses. These are diagnostic categories that are frequently used when there are no specific psychopathological grounds for another classification. Generally, you observe indications of severe mental imbalance, which in this case expressed itself in disturbed, excited behaviour, profound restlessness and unstructured thought processes. When I questioned the patient's wife, it emerged that he was a heavy drinker. Also, the death of a close relative was mentioned. Such factors may well have contributed to his severely disoriented state of mind."

"On the basis of what you know now, and given his mental condition, would you say that at the time of his referral to you for examination, he was in a position to understand his own actions and their consequences?"

"His state of mind – that is, his mental derangement – was without question causing him to be extremely agitated, unable to think clearly or to concentrate. He was only capable of answering a few questions, and then more or less at random. It was hard to connect with him at all. He sang, shouted and resisted the examination. Consequently, the patient had to be restrained to calm him down. At that point in time, he was not in a fit state either to control his behaviour or be aware of his actions."

"Is it possible that someone who has lost a close relative would react in this way?"

"Yes."

"Is it also possible that someone who has done a dreadful crime could also exhibit such behaviour when assailed by feelings of guilt and awareness of what he has done?"

"Conceivably, various stressful situations could trigger behaviour of this kind, but the present case does not fit this category. In practice, I'd say that cases of this kind have not yet been observed scientifically. Instead, it is far more common for the patient to first develop a psychotic condition and then go on to commit a crime or a punishable offence – and I say this as someone who has experience of working in a prison hospital with psychiatric patients who have committed criminal acts."

The psychologist is the first witness to appear to be quite untroubled by the questioning. He even seems to enjoy talking about his work. He looks at the prosecutor while he waits expectantly for the next question.

"Have you ever, in your personal experience, come across a patient who first commits a crime and then develops a mental illness?"

"In my prison hospital work, I've never come across an instance of a patient who first commits a crime and, in connection with that crime, later develops a psychotic condition. All my patients have either become psychotic and then committed the criminal act, or committed the act without suffering from psychotic incidents afterwards."

"Thank you, doctor. Now, Mrs Šimić has said about her husband, 'Ever since the war began, he has been anxious, tense and impatient.' Are you able to draw any conclusions from this? In other words, does this statement allow you to conclude that his psychotic condition had become manifest already before his admission to hospital?"

"No, not the psychosis. Certainly the overwhelming energy, the physical restlessness and the anxiety. I would agree that's likely."

"But, sir, there was a war on. Surely normal people were also exceptionally nervous and driven and irritable? In fact, isn't that a normal range of reactions in wartime?"

"Such reactions depend on personality. Some people are likely to become depressed, others aggressive and yet others, like this patient, hypomanic and exhibiting an overwhelming drive to take some action. Some people flee, some develop persecution mania and others cope with their situation and adjust to it – all this depends on factors in their personality and character. There are no rules for how people will behave in extreme or intolerable situations."

"Thank you, doctor. I would now like to ask you the following question: at the time the crime took place, was the defendant capable of distinguishing between right and wrong?"

"A joke has just come to mind, one I mustn't tell in a court of law. However, it's about two mentally ill persons discussing something and ends with one of them saying to the other: 'I might be mad, but I'm not stupid.' That is to say, even if he had been in a psychotic state at the time, this would not necessarily have caused him to be unaware that specific behaviour has moral implications."

"While he was treated under your supervision, did he ever seem to you to have lost the capacity for recognising the fundamental difference between right and wrong?"

"It's debatable. No one can be completely certain on this point, and besides, in psychiatry, we don't usually address the question of whether the patient is aware of the distinction between good and evil. We try to deal with disturbed and confused mental states. Once the patient is capable of behaving in a reasonable manner and controlling his impulses, and the psychopathological symptoms have faded into the background, then he is, in our opinion, cured and hence responsible for his actions."

"You describe the defendant at the time of his admission as agitated and out of control. He resisted you. Can you recall him speaking of a house going up in flames, or of dead people?"

"No, the only thing I can recall is this: he called out to someone by name. Over and over again he shouted, 'Gordana!' And, 'Let her go, set my Gordana free!' At least, this was the name he used, as I understood it. I asked him about this woman, you know, who she was and so on, but he didn't respond. He also called out, according to my notes: 'I'll grind your bones to dust, and make a paste of your blood, and of the paste a coffin.' At this point we had to restrain him physically. As I've said, he was very confused at the time."

He senses a hand touching his leg. It takes a moment before he realises whose hand it is. Aisha has taken her headphones off, points to his set and then whispers something he can't quite catch. She looks at him as if waiting for an answer. He can't work out what she wants.

"Hey, what's up?" she asks. "Are you coming or staying here?"

He gets up and, crouching, pushes his way past the others in the row. She follows him and, when they're both outside, asks what's wrong with him.

"Nothing."

"To me, you looked as if you weren't there at all. I was watching you and at times you were far away. Not in the same room any more."

He is relieved that she doesn't insist on an answer. While he thinks about what he can say, she turns and walks on ahead. He doesn't try to catch up with her on the staircase and has to hold onto the banister. He is convinced that Šimić shouted "Cordana", not "Gordana".

They walk towards the sea, along the road he took the first time he was in this city. He buries his hands in his coat pockets. They soon arrive at the bus stop where he sheltered on that first night. Aisha walks alongside him. Her head is slightly bowed. She is wearing a winter jacket which makes her look bulky, its zip pulled right up to her chin and her hands hidden inside its sleeves, as if her arms have been amputated.

He tries to listen to her footsteps, but can't hear a thing. He wonders about her ability to move so soundlessly, even though there is nothing light about her body, nothing to give her that ballerina-like weightlessness. She is hefty, unlike Ana who stepped so lightly she hardly touched the ground. Because of that silence, he turns to her and wouldn't be surprised to find that she has vanished. She raises her head and looks at him quizzically.

Blasts of cold wind buffet them as they come closer to the sea. He can't understand what they're doing there in this freezing weather. They struggle along the street until they reach the promenade with the wide beach stretching ahead and, beyond it, the sea, which is dark grey despite the blue sky.

"What now?" he asks.

"Isn't there some place to sit in the warmth and look at the sea?"

They go to the café he'd been to on the evening he went to the prison. They find a table in the conservatory. Aisha orders a pot of tea. "Don't you want anything?" she asks. He hesitates, then asks for tea.

They sit looking out over the sea.

"Why did you want to get out of there?"

She puts her hands on the table, one on top of the other, as if to warm them. "I just couldn't bear it any longer."

"How come?"

She stares at her hands.

"I couldn't take any more of the way they kept trying to find an explanation for why he did what he did. Psychosis, alcoholism, the death of his son – why try to understand what cannot be understood? It came across like they were trying to show how understanding they are. What a sad man, whose life was so thrown out of kilter that in the end they had to strap him to his bed. So what? Am I supposed to feel sorry for him?"

"But perhaps he really did experience something that threw him off balance."

"You mean the death of his son?"

"Perhaps something else, as well."

"Like what?"

"The war had reached Višegrad. Surely Serbs, too, might have suffered? Anyway, how can you be so certain that he's guilty?"

"How can you doubt it? Are you serious? Have you ever looked him at him properly? You must have seen the contempt he feels for everything? There he sits, all neatly buttoned up in his suit and his hair combed. He must be shaving every day, and probably reeks of aftershave. That's just perverse, when you think what he's charged with. If he were innocent, he wouldn't shave every morning, cool as anything, and worry about things like whether his suit is looking good. Just imagine yourself in his place, that you're accused of having caused the death of forty-two human beings – not just caused their death, but led them, the children and the babies too, into Purgatory – and you *know* you're innocent while everyone else thinks you're a murderer. Would you have the peace of mind to shave in front of the mirror every morning? In that situation, do you think you'd check that your suit was buttoned and that you smell nice? That man is a killer... no, he's someone worse than a killer, because he was too cowardly to do it himself and left the actual killing to others."

"How can you be so sure of your own judgement?" he asks.

"You've never been to Bosnia, have you?"

"No."

"Maybe you should go there some time. It might make you understand."

"What would I understand?"

"What it was all about."

"The problem is that here in Berlin, in Germany, people don't know what went on during the war. Their ideas come from a handful of images, like the emaciated men behind a barbed-wire fence. Or people running away from snipers. And so forth. Any judgement they make is going to be unreliable. It's like picking up a few pieces of a thousand-piece jigsaw, taking a look at them and then deciding you know the whole picture. If they'd seen different images, they might well have reached different conclusions."

This all came up the day after the supper at his best friend's place, when they were walking to Ana's flat.

"Do you know the truth about the photo showing emaciated men crowded behind barbed wire?"

"What truth?" he asked.

He knew that some kind of concentration camp had been constructed in Trnopolje and that these images, of a kind bred into the bone of German people, had caused huge outrage.

"These men weren't kept in a compound surrounded by barbed wire. The journalists had filmed an area of land with a barbed-wire fence. They deliberately made it look like a concentration camp. In the end, these concocted photos triggered NATO's intervention in the war."

This was the first time he heard this and, despite not wanting to, he doubted the truth of it. It disturbed him that he couldn't believe her.

"You know what it's like here," she said. "When people find out I'm a Serb, they think I'm fascist if I don't admit to my guilt or, at least, the guilt of my people. They've no patience with any 'buts'. And that hurts me, because it denies me my own life story, my experiences. And it provokes me too. I end up defending something that I don't want to defend in the slightest. And that's why I'd rather not discuss it."

At the time, he had no idea of how much she brooded about her own life story. That he did not now grieves him profoundly – and infuriates him too, because she doubted him for months. How else could he interpret his lover's silence? – her inability to talk about what troubled her for nine long months. The fact that she concealed her life could only mean that she couldn't trust him or let him come close. And what could have been her reason?

"Why are you here?" he asks.

Aisha sighs audibly. She keeps her eyes fixed on the shore where the twilight is deepening and blotting out the sea. Far away, near the horizon, lights are coming on, lights that don't move.

"I come from Višegrad," she says without looking at him.

He feels tenseness spreading through his body, his heart beats faster, his hands begin to shake and his thoughts become disordered, out of control.

"I was born there. I was fourteen when we fled."

He holds his breath, staring past her into the dusk. Then he briefly shuts his eyes, before asking her: "Do you know Ana?"

"Which Ana?"

"Ana Šimić."

His insides contract and he looks around to find something to hang on to. The picture on the wall behind Aisha. It's the same one as on the wall of his room in the guesthouse. He sleeps beneath this picture. He inspected it on his first morning and took in that image of a girl with her hair hidden under a turban, though one pearl earring was visible; she was looking at him wide-eyed with her lips slightly parted. His gaze travels to Aisha's jacket on the coat-rack, next to it hangs his own coat. The waitress is standing at the glass-covered counter, cautiously pushing a slice of chocolate gateau onto a plate. Then his eyes wander back to the picture. To the girl who, it seems and surely he can't be wrong, meets the onlooker's eyes with such expectation.

He hears Aisha ask a question.

"Is she his daughter?"

Aisha doesn't know her, and he isn't sure whether he's comfortable with this situation. Her voice has a new note in it, quieter, gentler. As if all her anger has been swept away.

"Yes," he says.

"And you know her?"

"I love her."

He holds his breath, stays still.

"Did you know she was his daughter?"

"No."

"When did you find out?"

"A few weeks ago."

"How did you find out?"

"I found his letters to her."

One morning, the letters were lying on her desk. He still doesn't know if she had forgotten them or left them there on purpose. He has often wondered about this. Was he meant to find them? This is what he has believed up till now. Several letters were stacked next to her computer. Not just one letter lying around, which would have been understandable. She might have read it the day before and simply forgotten to clear it away – not thought of him finding it. But a whole pile of letters on her desk could not be mere forgetfulness. When he walked over to the window in the morning, he saw them, some five or six letters. She wasn't in the room, so she must have been in the bathroom or the kitchen, although he cannot remember hearing anything. Usually, he would hear noises, like plates being put on the table or coffee gurgling in the coffee-maker. That morning, the flat was quiet.

He didn't want to read the letters, but it would be a lie to deny they aroused his interest. Standing at the window, he could not get them out of his head. He was curious about who had sent them. He remembers speculating that they might have been love letters. Fear paralysed him for a moment: was there perhaps another man in her life, someone who lived somewhere else? He tried to drive this notion away.

Who might have written to her? Her parents most likely. Letters from Višegrad. He wondered about possible letters from Višegrad, if they were sent by her father or her mother. What would the stamps be like? Then he could resist no longer: he returned to the desk and scrutinised the pile of letters.

He read her name and address; the rounded characters were in blue ink. The letters weren't addressed to Ana, but to Cordana. He recognised the handwriting, the way "Cordana" was written, almost like a loop that continued into an "a", then into a similar loop to end the name. It was her father's handwriting. It was the first time he saw her father's version of his surname. The "S", with exaggerated curves, the strangely minimised "i" without a dot, then the "c" on its own, with no connection to the rest. He kept staring at her name and, after what felt like an eternity, noticed "Nederland" on the stamps. He tried to make out the postmark. The date was indecipherable, but not the place. Scheveningen.

He picked up the letter on top of the pile and turned it round. There was no sender or sender's address. He scanned the other letters; no doubt about it, they were all from her father and all posted in Scheveningen. It didn't for a moment occur to him that her father might be in jail; he didn't link the place to the prison.

He felt annoyed. Ana had never mentioned that her father was in Holland. He had always assumed that her parents lived in Višegrad, now, as before. He couldn't think why she should have kept silent about it, not said that her father had been living in Scheveningen for some time. She had told him so much about her father. Why not this?

And why was he there? Maybe there was a simple explanation and he would accept it if she cosied up to him, put her arms around his neck and gave him a sideways glance with that sweet, girlish look in her eyes. Then his anger would seem over the top and he would simply have to forgive her. After all, there could be hundreds of reasons. But, secretly, he felt that this time there were no easy answers.

So what if she were to tell him that her father had fallen ill and found out that the best treatment was available in Scheveningen? Or that her father had gone there for a term's teaching? He would ask her why she hadn't mentioned it and she'd answer that it just didn't seem important enough at the time, or that somehow it slipped her mind. He could accept all that. Besides, why should it matter where her father was? That his parents lived near Hanover was something he had only recently got around to telling her.

He climbed back into bed and pulled the duvet tight. He wanted just a few more minutes in bed. They had made love that night. She had woken up first, and he felt her pressing close to him. She was kissing his chest, then put her hand between his legs. To him, no fantasy could be more exciting than being brought out of his sleep aroused and lying in the quiet darkness as lust pulsated in him. It was as if he had surfaced from deep inside his dreams to sense what being alive was like for a while, before immersing himself once more. He dozed off after their love-making. In the morning, the memory of something wonderful stayed with him, as if it were part of his dreams.

He had woken up in a good mood, unaware that he might have slept with her for the last time. He would often ask himself afterwards if she had known. If that night was her farewell gift to him. And if she knew it was, whether she found it wretched.

They had been to the cinema, come home late and gone to bed almost at once. Perhaps the pile of letters was already there, but he hadn't noticed them. The other possibility was that she had placed them there while he was asleep, during the night or the early hours of the morning. Or perhaps – he hadn't thought of this before – leaving them proved how much she trusted him and, as she saw it, was opening her life to him. But he didn't understand and didn't find the right response. He couldn't comprehend why she seemed so distant that morning.

She was dressed in jeans and a T-shirt when she came into the room.

"That was lovely," he said.

She stood next to the bed, looking down at him.

"I couldn't sleep," she said.

"Why not?"

"I don't know."

She went to open the window and glanced at the letters as she turned. She might have checked whether he had disturbed the pile.

"Your father has been writing to you," he said and paused. "How long has he been in Scheveningen?"

She only looked at him. Something about her reaction troubled him and suggested she might after all have left the letters on her desk quite unintentionally. She clearly felt under attack. Much later, he realised she had instantly assumed that he knew about her father being in the Scheveningen prison.

"Why haven't you told me?" he asked.

She stood with a hand on the letters, undecided what to say.

"Why is he there?" he asked.

Then she took one step away from the desk and their eyes met. He has never forgotten the look in hers and it frightened him. She stared intently, almost aggressively, at him. And in that moment, he had no idea why. He understood nothing.

"My father," she said and then stopped. "My father is charged as an accomplice to the murder of forty-two people. They were allegedly murdered in a house fire. According to public opinion, he's a war criminal. You have fallen in love with the daughter of a war criminal."

While she spoke, he was in the bed but must at some point have pulled himself up to lean against the wall, his torso was bare and he felt how cold his back had become. She met his eyes and seemed to expect something from him, but he couldn't respond. At the time, he thought that she must want to end things between them. Because there would have been other ways to tell him this. In bed, lying in his arms, for instance. But perhaps he wasn't quite ready to grasp how hard it was for her to tell him about this, especially him, who loved her, whom she loved. Surely she feared that he would fail to cope with her secret, that he would reject her. Perhaps she was proved right in the end. Didn't he leave her? Didn't he wait for her to make the first move?

She walked out of the room, as if in a hurry. Or so it seemed to him, because he felt that everything else stood still. He got up after a while, perhaps a long while, and attempted to pull his trousers on; he had to try three times before he could push his feet through the trouser legs because he kept losing his balance and had to sit down on the bed. He scanned the room to see if any of his things were still there. He spotted his socks on the floor next to the bed, together with the book by Ivo Andrić. He pulled his socks on and left the book. He stood up and went out of the room. A floorboard creaked under his weight. That was the only sound.

He remembers one passage in the book, where the Mullah Ibrahim says that one should not disturb flowing water, divert it and alter its bed in any way – not for a day or even an hour, because that would be a major sin. But the Swabian can't leave things alone; he has to hammer away and make things.

Aisha is studying him carefully. He doesn't expect her to understand. She just sits still, her palms pressed against her cup of tea.

"You should go," she tells him. "People like you, who haven't lived there, have only watched the war on TV, you can't understand what it's really like. I could never live with a Serb; I wouldn't do that to my family. People outside looking in might think that the war is over. Sure, when you travel in Bosnia, you'll still see houses that haven't been shot to bits, and you'll see people drinking in the evenings and going to work during the day, just like in any other country. But take a look at the bank notes. They're not the same, you see. Some are printed in Cyrillic script, some in the Latin, and on the first kind you'll see Serb heroes and on the second, Muslim ones.

You'll learn that the people who lived through that war lead two lives, the one they have during the day and the other one, which starts when they go to bed and try to sleep."

Meanwhile, the lights along the Promenade have come on. It is quiet out there beyond the windowpane. A vision of her lips comes into his mind, the tiny freckle she gave him, his *pega*. To him, she was the embodiment of stillness, of inner peace. He recalls the Serb word, it's *mir*, and means "stillness" but also "peace". Was he deceiving himself? How could he believe that someone who has lived through what Ana has lived through could ever achieve inner peace? What did it mean, to lead two lives? Has he no part in one of them? Could she ever share that one with him in any way? Share it with someone who hasn't experienced what she has, who cannot know what it's like to have two lives? In the beginning, she had perhaps hoped this was possible, but soon she realised that it wasn't. He felt excluded, behind glass, just like all those days in the court. Aisha has shown him that people like him can't understand people like her. Was there no way out? Was he destined to be an onlooker? Would he be forever analysing Ana's life, without being able to share it with her? He refuses to believe this. He will not allow himself to be locked out. Besides, who says that Ana and Aisha must be the same? Perhaps he really should go there.

"I'd really like to ask you something," he says. "I'd like to know if you've had a relationship."

"What do you mean? If I've been in love?"

"Yes."

"We met in Germany. He lived in the room next door, with his family. We shared the use of a bathroom and a kitchen. They had fled two week before us, from Goražde, which was besieged at the time."

"Why isn't he here?"

"He tries to draw a line under all that. He doesn't want to hear anything more about the war, he wants to … I don't know … at least separate the daytime from the wartime; he wants to enjoy the day."

"Do you talk about the war?"

"We did in the beginning. He told me what his family had to deal with, how they managed to flee, and I told him my story. We both know what it was like, so we no longer need to speak about it."

They had been in bed together so many times and, after putting away their books and switching off the light, these were the moments when he felt very close to her. Just the two of them, while the dark obscured everything else and perception depended on touch alone. The sensations of their bodies, their shared warmth under the duvet, her cold toes and hot belly. He felt that they trusted each other profoundly. And, so he thought, those were the moments when they should have talked. Now it occurs to him for the first time that the dark evenings in bed were not in fact suited to togetherness, because that was when she immersed herself in her other life.

"How long are you here for?" he asks Aisha.

"I was going to stay for a whole week, but I think I'll leave sooner. What about you?"

"Tomorrow morning."

"Will you come back?"

"I don't think so. Will you?"

"I want to be here for his sentence."

He wishes that he could have said the same, with the same clarity. But he's unsure of his own feelings. Inside him, an empty space is widening. The honest thing would be to admit that he can't be bothered with Šimić anymore. Somehow, his rage against this man, who has caused Ana so much grief, seems to have drained away.

"Would you like something else to drink?"

She shakes her head.

"Let's go, then. I'll walk you to the bus stop," he says. He waves to the waitress, finds some money in his trouser pocket and then asks the waitress how to get to the railway station.

It's almost eight o'clock now. Aisha can't hide how disconcerted she is by this sudden departure. He pushes his chair back to go, but she stays sitting at the table and takes a sip from her practically empty teacup.

Outside, it feels colder than before, even though the wind has died down. They both try as best they can to shield their faces behind the collars of their coats.

The day by the sea. He opened up the map, resting it on his knees. They had just left the seaside and settled into the car, waiting for it to warm up. He had turned the fan to the top setting. She warmed her hands between her thighs. He was so cold he could hardly move his fingers. "Where do we go now?" she asked. "Where would you like to go?" "Anywhere that's warm." "Back home?" he asked. "No, I don't want to go home," she answered. "Tell me where you'd like me to take you." "I don't know. Just drive."

"Thank you for coming with me," Aisha says when they arrive at the bus stop.

They stand there together, waiting for the bus. He can't think of the right way to say goodbye. Should he hold out his hand? Hug her? They are the only people around. There's a park on the other side of the road, and the naked branches of the trees stand out against the evening sky.

He hears her voice. She is saying that Lejla Hasan-ović was her best friend.

"We went to school together. The same age, you see. We lived just two houses apart. Our families had decided to go away together. It was all planned and we were waiting for Lejla and her family. The buses were ready and we were told we had to get on board; they couldn't wait any longer. I'm positive that my father went over to one of the organisers and told him that there were other people still to come, two more families, but the man told him that more transport would soon be coming. In the end, we boarded the bus. I only learnt what happened a year later. To this day, I agonise about Lejla and why she was so late."

He sees the headlights of the bus, hears the rumbling of the engine and the whoosh of the doors. As Aisha steps in, she turns and looks at him, but he can't interpret the expression on her face. It actually seems expressionless. He watches as she passes rows of seats and then settles by the window somewhere in the middle of the bus. The bus is ready to leave when he spots an elderly lady sitting next to the aisle, two rows behind Aisha. He's sure he recognises her and briefly considers knocking on the window, but only watches as the bus pulls away from the stop. Having taken a mental note of the illuminated number above the rear window of the bus, which has come from the prison, he checks the time and then the timetable. Departure 20.37. It's 20.39.

Ana, I often ask myself what you knew and how much you wanted to know. When did you learn about the charges against your father? Since then, have you looked him in the eyes? Questioned him? Perhaps it's mistaken to imagine that children, of all people, would want to know. Why would they want to shatter their cherished belief that their parents won't betray them?

So, going far away was perhaps the best thing you could do. I understand you. I probably would have done the same. Because it's utterly unimaginable – my own father. My Dad, who was lying close to me on the lawn and whose heavy breathing I can still hear. Your father, who rocked you on his knee, lectured you and pressed your head to his chest when you couldn't bear Romeo drawing his sword and cutting Tybalt down.

It's unimaginably tragic that you're probably the only one who knows why your father did what he did. You believe that he did it for you. Ana, you taught me about that passage, "I will grind your bones to dust, And with your blood and it, I'll make a Paste, And of the Paste a Coffin I will rear..." It's Titus Andronicus, who speaks of the revenge he will take for the violation of his daughter.

Ana, I don't know what happened, you never said, but I want to know, even if I find it almost unbearable. The mere thought of what might have been done to you is terrible. The whole time, I've been thinking about myself far too much, that much seems obvious now, after all these weeks. Have you secretly thought me egocentric?

Do you know what worries me? That I've noticed how much my self-made image of your father has been changing. I see him now with the acuteness of hindsight and it disturbs me a great deal, because it reveals the hollowness of one's certainties and convictions, the weakness of their links to experience. Ana, I fear for you. I need to hold you in my arms.

I sat and waited for you in front of your door. I wanted to tell you that I had been to The Hague and that I intended to go there once more. I'm not sure how long I sat there, staring at your name on the door. And I saw his name. Earlier, I always saw yours.

Then I heard you come upstairs the way you do, hardly seeming to touch the steps. Do you know, when I think about you I often see you dancing, hair held back by a ribbon, turning in the dance, and I watch the bones of your shoulders stretch your pale skin, your slender arms, you've pushed your hair behind your ears and you hold your head high. You dance in your parents' sitting room and I see you through the window.

You faced me and met my eyes. And I thought, now she'll disappear into her flat and close the door. But you sat down next to me on the step. There we stayed, for a while, without speaking. Then you said, not looking at me, "Give me a little more time." And although I wondered if there would ever be enough, I replied, "All the time in the world."

Aisha was right, leading two lives must be how it's done. How else could he explain that people went for evening strolls in the centre of Sarajevo, sat around chatting in the many cafés, watched football games, and laughed as if nothing bad had ever happened there.

He could see the Miljacka from his hotel room and could watch the sluggish brown water flow along its riverbed. There was a free bathing site just below his window, with two bright blue pools where children swam in the mornings, coached by a trainer with a piercing whistle, and where lots of people enjoyed themselves in the afternoon, their jolly shouting reaching his fourth-floor room. From up there, he could see the way the river sliced the city in two and five of the bridges linking the embankments. If he looked upwards, between all the buildings, he saw the hillsides covered with white crosses, visible signs of the past. There were whole rows of them in the cemeteries, entire fields of dead who lost their lives during the killing years of 1992 and 1993. He feared them, or rather, the proof that man had played God and interfered with the autonomy of life.

He had studied a grave marked with five white marble plaques, set side by side and each inscribed with the same surname, each with the same date of death. The tragedy involved the five different dates of birth: 23rd March1954; 7th February 1958; 8th July 1981; 12th December 1983; 3rd April 1986. The family was unknown to him, but he could not forget it. How then could those who had known the individuals ever forget? Further upriver where a small path followed the right bank and courting couples sat on seats shaded by beech trees or the stone parapet of the embankment, he observed the pock-marked walls of the houses, with their multitude of small craters, many holes large enough to put your hand inside, some the size of dinner plates. Among the scars of war, there were curtained windows and washing on lines slung between the balconies. How casually they lived with the traces of violence!

He'd been in Sarajevo for three days when, on one of his many walks through the city in the August heat, he'd got to know Alija, who was standing on one of the bridges, looking down on the Miljacka's rusty, muddy water as its barely discernible current flowed through the city. Apart from two anglers sitting on the riverbank and holding their lines, Alija seemed to be the only one who wasn't in a hurry.

The traffic on the bridge was piling up. He heard the horns and the screech of tyres. The first thing he noticed about the large, heavily built man near him was his strong hands, perhaps because of the way they gripped the balustrade. The man's shirtsleeves were rolled up and he wore dark glasses.

"The war began here, on this bridge," said the man. He'd looked up at man, who now slowly turned to face him.

"A peaceful anti-war demonstration had come this far, when a group of Serbs started shooting into the crowd from over there," the stranger continued and gestured at the opposite riverbank. "That's how the war started." He held out his hand and added, "I'm called Alija. Is this your first visit to Sarajevo?"

He nodded.

"Where do you come from?"

"Berlin."

"My wife loves Berlin. Some of her relatives live there." He laughed. "I remember Berlin all right. Especially Friedrichstraße, she was all over the place, out of one shop and into the next, while I tried to keep up and carry all the bags for her."

He learnt later that Alija was forty-six years old and had fought in the war. He was a Muslim. Alija spoke about the war with humour, which seemed almost obscene in the context. He said that he and his men had often been crying with laughter during the hours they spent in gun positions banked high with sandbags. For instance, did he know that, a short time before the outbreak of war, the city received a massive delivery of rice from China? Right in the middle of the war, the people of Sarajevo started up Bosnia's first ever sake brewery. And they ate rice every day. In the end, Alija begged his mother to please think of something else, because he couldn't stand the sight of any more rice. Then, one day, his mother served up green rice for his midday meal. She had coloured it with grass. There were dozens of anecdotes like that, he said, and what they all did was make the war appear surreal. How could anyone laugh at civil war? Well, Alija managed, at least at times. Perhaps it was his way of keeping terror at bay.

They arranged to meet that evening in a restaurant on the riverside. They sat outside, watching the traffic on the opposite bank. He asked Alija if he had understood what the war was about.

"Some of it, yes. Some things are pretty much inexplicable."

Alija spoke of one of his Serb friends. They had lived in the same building and grown up together. His friend's father was in the army and had warned them that something was about to happen, several days before the outbreak of war. Then, suddenly, his friend was nowhere to be seen. Next, he phoned and told Alija to leave the city. When Alija asked where he had gone, the friend told him that they were encamped near the peak of the mountain. From up there, they were shooting at Sarajevo, at his own city. Later, he had called again and Alija asked how he could bring himself to shoot at the city where they had grown up and made friends. To shoot at those like Alija who still lived down there. His friend said that he had to do what he had to do. "Can anyone understand that?" Alija asked. "Try as I may, I never can."

Alija drank beer and ate šiš kebap, Turkish-style. "Our traditional fare," he said with a laugh. He pointed at a large building on the other side of the river. The facade had been handsome, with glazed brick arches and decorative pillars, but a gaping tear in the wall exposed the interior. "That's the City Library," Alija said. "They were ordered to destroy it. Who gave the order? A professor at the university here, who served as a high-ranking officer in the Bosnian Serb forces during the war."

He couldn't help thinking of Šimić, who had taught here. Should he ask Alija about him? But he wasn't sure what to say when Alija asked him, as he would, why he was so interested in Šimić. They sat in silence, looking out over the river. Folk music drifted across the water from a restaurant at a bend of the Miljacka. A little later, as he poked about in the small earthenware pot his šiš kebap was served in, he asked his question. Alija looked at him quietly for a moment and then replied: "Yes, I've heard of him. One of my friends was a student of his."

They met up with Alija's friend for lunch the following day. Twenty years earlier, he had spent a couple of terms taking Šimić's classes. He said that Šimić was very well liked by the students. He was a gentleman. Always courteous, he would hold the door open for students and didn't rush individual tutorials. Once a month, he would meet up with his students in some bar or other; he loved jazz, and John Coltrane in particular.

They were in Sarajevo's old quarter, in a Turkish café with a view of the main mosque's minaret. The seating was on low benches covered with brightly coloured cushions. While Alija stirred his mocha with a tiny spoon, he translated what his friend was saying.

Apparently Šimić usually wore a tweed jacket with leather patches on the elbows and his sense of humour favoured Harold Pinter, whatever that was supposed to mean. Šimić had written several books about Shakespeare and then, just before the war, another one about his own ideas concerning nationhood. And that book, the friend said, seemed to have nothing to do with the man he had known. Something must have happened to Šimić.

A few days later, Alija got hold of a copy of the book and also translated some passages for him. In one essay about Shakespeare, Šimić argued that every major character would reach a point beyond which life itself was worth less than the greater purpose around which the play revolved. He went on to single out the heroes of Kosovo as the architects of their own deaths, asking if this should not be seen as the ultimate goal of all heroic figures in tragedy, from Homer to Shakespeare. Was that what he wanted? To be the architect of his own destiny?

Alija's friend recalled that Šimić had worn a black ribbon for two whole years after the death of his son. "It could be that his son's death changed him utterly."

In the evenings, they would spend time together at a British pub, high up on one of the hills. The pub belonged to one of Alija's acquaintances. They often sat in the beer garden looking out over the hilly cityscape that rose above the Miljacka. Late in the evening, all they could see were the lights shimmering against the warm night sky, and they would chat in low voices, even though they were outside. Only the children were still noisy, shouting gleefully as they ran around between the tables. He can no longer remember why, but one evening they started to talk about love. Alija asked if he loved someone. He nodded, imagining that Ana was sitting next to him in this company, watching the lights of the city, which seemed to speckle the sky.

In the night air the outline of the mountains could be clearly seen. How fateful the city's location had proved to be: the mountains had trapped the people in Sarajevo.

He asked Alija if he could imagine falling in love with a Serb woman. "No," he replied and his friend added: "The relationship wouldn't stand a chance." He later learned that the friend and his family had been driven out of Pale.

"There's something stronger even than love and that's the memory of the past."

Did any of this matter to him? Should their memories come between Ana and himself? He stared at the mountains, trying to conjure up images of tanks lined up on the heights, of guns shooting at the city indiscriminately. These were not his images.

The next day, they went for a short tour by car, taking the eastern exit from the city, passing Pale and turning in the direction of Višegrad. They drove past the rich, green meadows of the softly rising hills and up into the mountains. Later, the road was flanked by forests stretching all the way to the horizon on both sides. Houses were a rare sight in these hills. He was reminded of all the times in his childhood his parents had taken him walking in the Bavarian Voralpenland. He hadn't expected this magnificent hill country.

The road climbed steeply upwards through dense forest. The car windows were open and the shade of the trees cooled the air. After crawling for a while behind a lorry, they reached the top of the pass and began the descent. The view ahead was so unforgettably beautiful that he almost asked Alija to stop for a moment.

They were about to cross a plateau, which seemed utterly untouched, a soft, green expanse as smooth as the surface of a still sea and too wide for him to see where it ended. They drove through a small village, a group of just three or four houses. A girl herded a couple of cows. Elderly people sat on their verandas and watched the cars on the road. Behind the houses, men were out cutting the meadow grass with their scythes. He saw all this and listened as Alija told him of the massacres that had been carried out in these hill villages, of how people had been crowded together in a field and shot. Blood had soaked into this rich soil, but he couldn't imagine it. Still, on the way back, he saw the men wielding their scythes in a new light.

The war had not been between Muslims and Serbs, Alija told him. City people had fought the population in the countryside. "Urban versus rural," he added in English. The farmers had been the first group to take to killing. Slaughter had been part of their lives, so when it was suddenly a matter of killing human beings rather than animals, they adjusted quickly. Easy enough, if you already have blood on your hands. It soon reached biblical proportions.

Alija asked if he knew the story of Abraham. The point, he said, was that Abraham was willing to kill his own son. Those who fought here sacrificed their blood for this land – well, for the Serb nation. But a nation is only an abstract concept which translates as the ground around your home, the place where you're born, the land providing the harvests that keep you alive, the landscape of your songs and the wild beauty described in your poetry. The people here fought and died willingly for love of their homeland. It was their form of heroism.

Then the landscape changed again, as abruptly as when the plateau had opened up in front of them. From nowhere, steep, bare rock faces emerged on every side and towered high up above them as the road wound its way through gorges. The murmur of flowing water came through the open windows when the road began to follow the course of a stream. Here and there, it widened into small pools. People were out fishing and Alija told him that the streams around those parts were teeming with fish.

It took almost three quarters of an hour on that mountain road before they entered a wide river valley. The river water was an intense green, which seemed to glow where the sun caught the surface. He breathed in deeply, trying to control his excitement. There it was, the Drina, on the floor of a valley whose gently increasing gradient stretching to the mountains gave it the form of a bathtub.

They followed the river for a while, then parked the car by the roadside and took a path leading down its bank. Someone had cut steps into the ground. Just twenty, maybe thirty metres along, they entered a small wood where the water glinted through the undergrowth. The well trodden path ended at a clearing around a shed. Plastic bottles, tied to tree branches, floated in the water. In front of the shed, a ramp sloped into the Drina. The brown riverbed was clearly visible through the water.

He crouched and immersed his hand, then looked at it as if Drina's waters would leave traces on his skin. "Did you ever go swimming in the Drina?" he asked Alija.

"As a child. Not since the war. The river is poisoned now."

During the onward journey, which took them through several tunnels, he couldn't take his eyes off the river. The plastic rubbish it carried downstream was a disappointment – mainly bottles and bags. At one point, he spotted what he thought was the floating carcass of some animal, maybe the bloated body of a goat or a large dog. It drifted slowly.

Another half an hour and then, after a bend in the river, the valley widened and they saw houses on the opposite shore for the first time. They were empty. "And, as you can see, gutted by fire," Alija said. He looked more closely and realised that the roofs were only beams and the windows no more than gaping holes in the stone-work.

The many-arched bridge could be seen from far away. He had imagined it would look more vulnerable, like other long bridges. But this bridge was different, its solidity obvious even from a distance. It didn't so much span the water as just stand there, as if it had been standing there when the waters first arrived, as much a part of the landscape as the mountains. A bridge for all time.

He tried to recall this passage from Ivo Andrić's book:

How can they describe that surge within a man that passes from dumb animal fear to suicidal ecstasy, from the lowest impulses of bloodlust and pillage to the greatest and noblest of sacrifices, wherein he momentarily touches other spheres, higher worlds with other laws? Never can this be told, for those who have seen and lived through such things have lost the gift of words and those who are dead tell no tales. Those are things that are not told, but forgotten. For were they not forgotten, they surely would never be repeated?

They parked and walked towards the bridge. When they reached it, Alija stopped and leaned on the stone balustrade, looking down into the water. Then he waved to him to come closer. He went over to see what Alija was pointing to. In the shade of the piers, large dark fish had gathered close to the surface of the water. They seemed suspended there, using just one or two flicks of their tailfins to stay effortlessly still, despite the rushing currents forming on either side of the stone columns of the bridge.

"They can grow half a metre long, you know," Alija told him.

He laughed.

"Hey, that's no joke," Alija said.

"When were you last here?"

"It was years ago. There's nothing here for Muslims anymore."

There were just a few others on the bridge. An old man stood with his face turned to the sun. A couple took photos of each other in the central area with the stone seat, where men had met for hundreds of years to play cards, talk and argue.

Once the couple had left, Alija leaned against the wall at the end of the stone bench they called the *kapija*. "This is where they were lined up. Their throats were cut before they were thrown into the water. One after the other. Hundreds of them. Executed by their own neighbours. So what do you see here? A memorial? Some kind of plaque? Nothing would seem to have happened here. Look, at the mosque there," he said and pointed to the minaret which towered over the roofs of the houses. "They've even rebuilt that. But Muslims don't live here anymore."

Only a year earlier he would have strolled across this bridge and seen just an ancient and majestic bridge. He would have been awed by its structure and historical significance, and enjoyed the view of the river. He might actually have sat down on the stone bench, perhaps relaxing against the stone armrests. He felt ashamed at the thought of his past ignorance. Alija seemed to sense what was going through his mind.

"These are not your memories," he said. "You lead your own life, deal with your own sorrows."

As they stood together and leant against the balustrade, they watched the flowing waters below. He could see the dark shapes of the fish. A couple of boys were swimming, supported by huge inflated inner tubes. Then he looked up at the mountains.

"One watches what's happening on the TV and does nothing. It's not right," he said.

"That's how it has to be," Alija replied. "We do it all the time."

On one of the left bank tennis courts, two girls were having a game. They listened to the sound of balls toing-and-froing between their rackets.

"At first, when the war had just started, we expected help from the outside world. We couldn't believe that what was happening here would be allowed to go on. But then the day arrives when you realise that this is your fate and that there's no point in waiting for someone else to intervene. It's up to you and no one else."

In the newly built café on the other shore, the out-door tables behind a low stone wall had a view of the river. Some were occupied: at one, two elderly ladies chatted over cups of coffee, at another, a woman cradled her baby while a man was on the phone. A couple sat on a bench with their arms around each other. The woman's eyes were closed and she leaned her head on the man's shoulder. The sun shone on their faces.

They lingered on the bridge for a while before walking back to the car. As they drove through the town, Alija pointed to a house near a small stream – or to what was left of it. The ruined walls were blackened by fire.

Epilogue

Today, the verdict has been reached in the case of defendant Zlatko Šimić.

The defendant was charged with personal criminal responsibility for the murder of forty-two Muslims, on the understanding that he, as defined in paragraph 7, clause 1 of the statutes, conspired in a joint criminal enterprise to murder this group of people. For the defendant to be deemed responsible as described, the prosecution must prove that he had entered into an agreement with the group led by Milan Marić to kill these people, and that every single participant in the enterprise, including the defendant, intended to commit this crime. However, the prosecution was unable to convince this court either that the defendant had entered into such an agreement, or that he intended to take the lives of these people.

As has already been established, the charge does not rest on the wider effects of the joint criminal venture, so the defendant cannot be held responsible for the natural and foreseeable consequences of any joint criminal undertaking in which he may have committed a less serious crime by participating in it. The prosecution was therefore unable to establish proof of the defendant's participation in a joint criminal enterprise to murder the Muslims locked into the House by the Stream in Pionirska Street.

The prosecution also charged the defendant with personal criminal responsibility for the murder of forty-two persons, on the basis that he assisted and collaborated with the leading perpetrator of this mass murder. In order to establish the defendant's responsibility as accomplice and collaborator of the chief perpetrator, the prosecution is obliged to provide evidence that the defendant was aware of the perpetrator's intentions and that the defendant's actions aided and abetted the crime as planned by the chief perpetrator, constituting a fundamental contribution to it. This court would find it credible that the defendant's efforts contributed to the cohesion within the group and hence to the execution of the crime as intended by the chief perpetrator, but is not however convinced that the defendant was aware of the perpetrator's intention, that is, the intention to murder the Koritnik group. It cannot therefore be proven that the defendant was criminally responsible for the murder of the Koritnik group, acting in the role of accomplice and collaborator.

The defendant is therefore found not guilty on the count of murder as stated in item ten of the charge, and not guilty on the count of being an accomplice to the murder as stated in item eleven of the charge.

ngelings other changelings other changelings other changel

Alessandro Barbero's *The Anonymous Novel*

About the book

Set in Gorbachev's Russia, this complex but highly readable novel not only provides the portrait of a society in transition, but also fascinating studies of various themes including the nature of history and the Russian novel itself. Barbero uses his skills as a historian to study the reality of Russian society through its newspapers and journals, and his skills as a novelist to weave a complex plot – a tale of two cities: Moscow and Baku. And throughout, the narrative voice – perhaps the greatest protagonist of them all – represents not the author's views but those of the Russian public as they emerged from one dismal reality and hurtled unknowingly towards another.

Comments

"In the depiction of these changing times, Barbero's political intelligence is apparent. So, however, is his skill as a novelist, for he contrives to integrate the socio-political analysis in his story of imagined characters. It never obtrudes itself; yet you can't ignore or forget it... If you have any feeling for Russia or the art of the novel, read this one. You will find it an enriching experience." – *The Scotsman*

"He writes in a bright and breezy, satirical style ... which leads the reader to believe that some Russian master has been leaning over his shoulder, guiding his hand... It is a deeply rewarding pleasure to be lost in this novel." – *The Herald*

"Barbero uses the diabolic skills of an erudite and professional narrator to seek out massacres of the distant and recent past. *The Anonymous Novel* concerns the past-that-never-passes (whether Tsarist or Stalinist) and the future that in 1988 was impending and has now arrived." – *Il Giornale*

"Alessandro Barbero's *The Anonymous Novel. Sensing the Future Torments*, from a new publisher, Vagabond Voices, situated on the Isle of Lewis, is a vivid novel about Russians coping with the transition from communism to capitalism and combines echoes of Bulgakov with elements of a thriller." – *The Observer*

Price: £14.50   ISBN: 978-0-9560560-4-7   pp. 464

Ermanno Cavazzoni's *The Nocturnal Library*

About the book

Ermanno Cavazzoni admits that his books push the novel to its very limits – "like outpourings of the maniacal," he says. "That's how they come to me, you must understand."

Here in The Nocturnal Library, we have the maniacal we all know from our own dreams: a dreamer's lack of control and a dreamer's dogged acceptance of the absurd. Here we have the dream as paranoia and the vain struggle to understand the rules that govern life. Here we have the dream as a bizarre library in which the fragility of human knowledge is emphasised again and again.

Jerome, who perhaps represents the archetypal man of learning, is bound up in his world of books and suffers from crippling insomnia. He has to study for an exam, and his troubles are compounded by a bad toothache, or at least these are the dominating themes of his dream. The reality of wakefulness only appears in the last paragraph of the last chapter.

But this is not primarily a book about dreams. Amongst other things, it is a book about the arrogance and illogicality of power and bureaucracy, and the relationship between the world of intellectual order and the chaos of nature, dominated as it is by mutual disregard and the latter's inevitable victory in the long term.

And above all, this is a book in which fantasy reigns for its own sake and goes wherever the author's creative impulse takes it. That is how his novels come to him, and you have to understand that! If you do, you will enjoy this exotic book.

Ermanno Cavazzoni's first novel was made into Fellini's last film, The Voice of the Moon.

Price: £12.50   ISBN: 978-0-9560560-5-4   pp. 224